John Rock

the world's most wanted man

Dedication

For Courtney.

Also for the three screwballs who inspired the John Rock character.

I'd like to acknowledge Rhia and Anthony for their proofreading and feedback on the novel and also Clarke for his feedback.

Table of Contents

Chapter 1

Two humanitarian aid workers huddled on their boat as it churned up a river. Their captain was going to put them in touch with a living legend. They were searching for John Rock, the dangerous ex-soldier they had been told could help them rescue their kidnapped colleague. He was the US military's most hated man and nobody knew why. It was rumored he had betrayed his country.

Charlie wrapped his arm around Joanna and they shielded themselves from the splashes of the boat. They had been near Pulai two days before, sleeping in their tents outside of Blue Hospice Field Hospital, when an armed rebel group shattered the peace of the night. A rebel leader had grabbed Gemma from her cot by her hair and hauled her to the Jeeps where his men waited, their heavy machine guns trained on the inhabitants of the camp. This was the last either Joanna or Charlie had seen of Gemma.

They had tried calling the American embassy and their Blue Hospice Relief headquarters to try and get some help but no one had been willing to do so. "You were told to leave the conflict zone," was the response they had received. So, they turned to local help and were now seeking out their final hope of rescuing a woman they'd known as a friend and confidante for the last two years of the unofficial conflict raging in the region.

John Rock was a whisper on the wind to the locals, a name uttered only after many, many drinks. The rebel groups steered wide of his rundown plantation on the shores of the Danta. On rare occasions it was mentioned that a fisherman would motor up the river and drop off supplies on a dock and retrieve an envelope. The envelope was filled with money that no one else dare take as their own. Charlie and Joanna had bickered over the dangers of looking for the man of mystery, but in the end Joanna's will and the drive to help Gemma convinced them to take the considerable risk. It was a last-ditch effort.

The trip up the Danta took the better part of a day. At several points, the fisherman warned the aid workers to stoop down so as to not be seen by various rebel groups camped out along the river. Mosquitos swarmed in the thousands overhead. The night air was only slightly less oppressive than the day's air had been. At long last, the boat bumped gently into a worn down dock. It had been several hours since they had last seen another human being. The fisherman, assisted by Joanna and Charlie, unloaded several barrels of supplies and tethered two goats to a post near where he had set several hens in cages. "Leave you here," was all that the fisherman said before speeding back down the river. He did not look back.

"Wait!" cried Joanna. "Ugh! He didn't say how long we would have to wait. This could just be a dead end."

"Shh. Just hold on, Honey. This guy's supposed to be the real deal. Let's stay here for a while and see if anyone turns up," said Charlie. He took a drink from a plastic water bottle and offered it to his fiancé.

They waited and waited until finally, they fell asleep.

When they woke up, they were laying in hammocks in a grass-thatched hut. Charlie could see ants crawling on the ground carrying shavings of fruit back to their hills. He gazed up at Joanna's lean and tanned figure for several moments before the jungle air caused him to clear his throat. Joanna rubbed her eyes and groaned. Neither of them remembered being taken to this hut. They made eye contact and sat up. The chopping of a machete could be heard a few meters beyond the walls of their hut. Charlie was the first to step out, donning his wristwatch and Northwestern University tee shirt. He winced at the glare of the morning light.

"Hello?" he called to the man who was standing with his back turned to them. Charlie felt very unsure of himself and the situation they were in. The man was heavily built and tan with long, ruddy blonde hair reaching down to the middle of his back. He was extraordinarily tall. A red bandana was tied around the crown of his head and a pair of black jeans hugged his legs. He paused from hacking at a coconut and grunted before returning to his work.

"Do you think that's John Rock?" whispered Joanna.

"I don't know."

The man finished chopping at the coconut and began carving at a pineapple. Soon he was gathering eggs and walking out of sight. Charlie and Joanna followed. The beaten footpath they rounded led them to another clearing. The man they had followed was nowhere to be seen.

"You must be the two humanitarian aid workers who are looking for some help," a voice came from behind them. Joanna let out a small cry and Charlie put his arm around her. They turned to see a short man "probably shorter than Jo", according to Charlie's mental guess. The man had a speckled hen under his arm. His hairy hand was stroking the hen across her back.

"Hi. I'm John Rock," said the man, much to the surprise of his guests.

He was wearing a burgundy collared shirt that was neatly tucked into perfectly pressed khaki pants. On his feet were thin, colorful sandals with a variety of straps crisscrossing in a confused medley. Bright white skin could be glimpsed beneath the sandal straps. The man held out his free hand to Charlie and shook it while giving him a firm look. John then quietly nodded at Joanna as though she were about to tell him a lusty secret. He did not offer her his hand. Joanna felt uncomfortable and looked away from his gaze.

"We're glad to meet you. I'm Charlie and this is Joanna," said Charlie.

"That's great. You guys must have heard a lot about me. I can get your friend back for you but it's going to be a tough case. Mutobo is a fierce leader and his rebel group isn't going to just give her up."

"How did you know about our friend?" asked Joanna while continuing to avoid eye contact.

"How do you know the name of the rebel who took her?" Charlie piped in almost at the same time.

John gazed his eyes back toward Joanna's figure, letting them study the slender contours of her breasts and hips. Joanna crossed her arms and shifted uncomfortably. He set the hen down and slowly stood back up. His body movement seemed calculated to his potential clients.

"Mutobo's an infamous rebel leader. Who doesn't know him? Besides, people tell me things. His hold-up at your camp was quite the little story up here. As for how you got here..." John whistled loudly. "Arnold *–fweet–come* here!"

A loud crashing came through the bamboo and into the clearing. It was the man with the machete Joanna and Charlie had seen earlier. Seeing him from the front allowed them to notice that something wasn't quite normal or healthy in his facial features. Arnold lumbered toward them with his machete and Charlie squeezed his arm even tighter around Joanna.

"He's harmless. Don't worry" cooed John. "Arnold. Introduce yourself and then go make our guests some breakfast."

Arnold held out his hand to Charlie, pulled it away before Charlie could hold his out in return, and then nodded in the general direction of Joanna. He lumbered away, breathing heavily through his mouth.

"Is he okay?" asked Joanna.

"Of course he's okay! He's had a cold lately. I think he fell asleep out with the pigs a couple nights ago. Arnie's good help around here. He's my apprentice now. We used to serve together a few years back. He helped me get out of the military when things went sour. I'm helping him become more authentic. We go way back. You're lucky you got to meet him."

John paused to run a hand through his hair.

"Most of the time he's off in the jungle picking mushrooms. Come, let's talk business in my hut and we'll get some breakfast in you two."

The overwhelmed pair followed John through the jungle compound to his hut. Along three of the walls of the hut were the heads of some of the world's largest predators, mounted on plaques commemorating the date of each kill. A corner of the small hut featured a pedestal that held tall, half-melted candles and an effigy of a futuristic helmet that was unrecognizable to the two guests. Next to the religious display lay a grass mat woven with intricate designs and skillful precision. Lying upon the grass mat was a bewildered looking gray cat that scattered out a back window the moment he set eyes on the two strangers. Charlie thought he glimpsed some cables and a video display in the back room before John stepped into the doorway to watch the cat run away.

"Rupert!" John called to the creature. "Oh, you guys would love Rupert. He's a rascal. Please, have a seat."

"Do you know where Gemma is being kept?" Charlie wanted to get straight to business.

"Gemma-" John paused, "that's a pretty name. I do know where she's being kept, at least, if I remember Mutobo (which I do). He'll probably be keeping her in his camp."

"Where's the camp?"

"About 80 clicks west from here, almost on the other side of the mountains. It's a pretty easy hike, should take less than a couple days. We can catch a ride for part of it. Can you tell me more about your friend, *Gemma*?" John said her name with special care while looking at Joanna.

Arnold trudged into the hut with a tray carrying plates of scrambled eggs, fresh pineapple rounds, and a halved coconut for each of the three to drink.

"Arnold, take the pineapple away please. You know I'm watching my insulin levels," John said with a roll of his eyes. He whispered to his new companions, "He doesn't always have a lot of Self energy. He forgets things sometimes. Anyhow, *Gemma*: tell me about her."

"She's been our friend for a while, our best friend in Pulai. We can pay you 70,000 renminbi to help us save her. It's all we have," Joanna pleaded.

"No, no, no. I mean, what does she look like?" Rock answered.

"Um…"

"I don't need your money, I have all the money I need and then some. I want to know what she looks like."

"John, I don't know if…"

"Come on," he urged her.

"Well, she has short, blonde hair in a kind of a pixie cut and is a little over five feet tall. She has freckles and a scar on her left shoulder."

"Nice. I love pixie cuts."

"What?"

"It's not important. Neither is your money. After earning a Purple Heart for heavy action in the roughest combat zone of Bogro, I won the lottery. Now I live here with my apprentice and our cat. My life is peaceful and simple but I have been out of the game wa-a-a-ay too long and I'm getting hungry again. I'm willing to do this one for free but-"

"Oh! Thank you, Mr. Rock! That's very noble of you," cried Joanna.

John took a deep breath in and his eyes rolled into the back of his head as he closed them. "I'd prefer you didn't interrupt me."

There was a moment of silence before he continued.

"We're going into hostile territory and Mutobo's men aren't exactly pussycats. I have a lot of emotional mastery that I can bring to this situation, plus all my tactical training, so I'm actually really glad you came to me. You'll have to give me the credibility that I know what I am doing *at all times*" John heavily stressed the last three syllables, "-cause trust me, it's gonna' get rough out there. Who knows? If we make it out of this one alive, we could end up becoming good friends," he chuckled. "Arnold! Boil me some eggs and pack some jerky. I'm gonna' be gone for a little while. You're gonna have to take care of the place till I get back."

Charlie and Joanna were too uncomfortable to say anything as John spent the next hour detailing a map for their trek to Mutobo's camp on a whiteboard.

Chapter 2

"Boy! Fetch me some water. I am thirsty now," called Mutobo to a young rebel posted outside of his hut. Mutobo paced from one end of the hut to another.

"Let us go over this again. Ms. Gemma Wayne, you have been stationed in Pulai as part of the United Nations effort to support General Utility, the Zabonese despots in power, and their plan to flood this valley with the dam they are building 30 kilometers from here, are you not? This is what my men have told me. This is what my dossier on your activities tells me. What do you say to this, huh?" Mutobo's massive frame towered over the bound humanitarian aid worker, his thick arms and forearms rippled as he spoke.

"I am a relief worker working for Blue Hospice. I was trained in the United States as an EMT and volunteered to come to the Danta region two years ago as part of UN Relief. What more can I tell you?" said Gemma. Her demeanor was nonchalant and almost coy, as though she was unconcerned with the bristling Mutobo.

"You are a liar!" yelled Mutobo. "I have seen you on reconnaissance with my own two eyes. We have pictures of you," he slammed down two large photographs onto the table to which Gemma was tied. "Here and here! This is you with an AK-47 you took from one of my men as a trophy. You are a known terrorist in the valley. How can you lie? We know you are UNSCA."

"What difference does it make to you? I am a relief worker."

"Nonsense, I will not stand around while you pretend you are some sort of doctor!"

He calmly put a gag into her mouth. The young rebel came back into the hut with a pitcher of water.

"Ms. Wayne, we have been good to you, have we not? You have not been punished, you have not been violated. All I am asking is that you admit your involvement in this situation. I am asking you to admit your crimes. I know you work for the United Nations. I am no fool. I am going to take off your gag in one hour. We will bring you water and a good meal. My men will treat you well but we have been here too much time, playing this game with you. We know your organization has disavowed you. You could spend many months on this mountain with no one to come for you. I am leaving." He turned to leave. "Boy, send for Alistair to cook some lunch for our guest, help him with what he needs. Then come back here and make sure she stays put."

Mutobo left the hut to confer with Walter, his second in command. Mutobo's rebel group had a firm grip on the Danta Valley but its power faded at Pulai. Mutobo led with reason and evidence. The greatest struggle of his life had not come from the years of civil war nor the trials he faced in piecing together his band of rebels. His greatest struggle had come from the effort he expended, with Walter's help, in inspiring the hearts and minds of his countrymen. He was uniting them in an effort to oppose the massive affront to life in the Bura and Danta that General Utility and the tyrannical Zabonese government represented.

General Utility, the largest energy corporation on the continent, had declared it was in negotiations with the Zabonese government to bring a massive hydroelectric dam to the Bura, a river running adjacent to the Danta Valley. The UN had overstepped the bounds of its stated mission by engaging in raids on locals. Its officials asserted the raids were part of a plan to capture "domestic terrorists".

Mutobo had no idea he had international renown as a mastermind terrorist. This lack of perspective was both a great charm for locals in the region and a great weakness when it came to maintaining funding. Hundreds of thousands of international fans sought to donate to his campaign because they loved his underdog status. They had no means of getting this money to him. Mutobo was oblivious. His concept of the world entailed what was directly in front of him and nothing else. The younger rebels in his group considered him a xenophobe.

Gemma Wayne divided her time between her UN post of "Head Intelligence Officer" and her humanitarian cover at the hospital. Given the recent oil boom in Zabon, Gemma had had no problem blending in with the mass of poor North Americans and Europeans who had flooded into the capital city of Pulai to take advantage of the lucrative oil and engineering positions available. In keeping with the mission objective of disrupting local support for the rebel groups and intercepting raid parties before they pillaged incoming aid, Gemma was stationed in the Blue Hospice Field Hospital by her commanding officer. Her cover was a volunteer EMT, but her real work was to gain the trust of wounded rebel soldiers and subsequently, their prized information. With the second highest rank of the Pulai field office and peacekeeping base, she had gained a large measure of control over the UN ground forces in the region. She took advantage of the shoddily pieced together operation by blackmailing anyone within sight. Her boss, Commander Sutherland, would not allow her to drop her cover at the hospital.

Word had spread of a blonde-haired female officer whose brutality during interrogations left men crippled and deeply scarred. One of these men had sought care at Blue Hospice and glimpsed the undercover intelligence officer as he hobbled out of the facility. Mutobo's agents were the first to know.

Mutobo walked between the camouflaged tents, small metal buildings, and mud huts of his makeshift compound to the Walter's tent. The two men had been friends since childhood and had watched as several other foreign interventions in the region had taken the lives of their friends and family. The second Zabon - Bogro War and the ensuing American intervention in recent years had been particularly brutal to their loved ones.

"Walta', you cannot believe this woman. I showed her the pictures Young Johnny took of her at the Tamil Bridge ambush. She just stared at me," Mutobo groaned as he ducked into the tent. He sat at a desk in the center of the room. Maps and laptop computers were strewn about. A large stack of philosophical works sat on a shelf next to loaded pistol.

"We have all the time in the world. She has been disavowed. Relax." Walter stood up and patted the shoulder of his massive friend.

Walter wore a speckled beard on a rugged face that held calm warmth in its cheeks. He was not nearly as large as his best friend but his eyes were just as sharp. Sleek reading glasses clung to the edge of his nose. On the black skin of his arms were cigarette burns from a Dutch soldier of fortune that had abused Walter as a young boy when he was a servant at an embassy manor.

"Thank you, man. You are right. We have time. Alistair is cooking her some lunch. If I were a weaker man, I would have slapped her, oh my God. I'll go back later." Mutobo leaned back in his chair with a smile and Walter returned to his computer.

Soon they were playing cards, smoking cigars, and laughing. They had not suffered any casualties in three weeks. Young Johnny had, in fact, recruited over a dozen new rebels to their ranks. They toasted to the health of the new recruits and to the prized capture of the UN's second in command. Their opposition of the Bura Valley dam project was rapidly gaining support. Thanks to the drop in violence, Mutobo was looking forward to visiting with his wife and daughter soon.

Chapter 3

Rupert stalked a mouse up into the innards of a rusting and broken down Jeep in the brush outside of the plantation. The mouse had been gnawing on a corn husk and was lucky enough to be facing Rupert's direction when the cat rounded a corner and came into view from a dimly-seen distance. After being frozen in place for a short moment by something unseen, the mouse had taken off with a noticeable limp. Their natural struggle had reached unfamiliar ground. Rupert crouched down to wait out his prey. The mouse was a stranger to Rupert, but the mouse, as well as every other creature on the plantation, had known of the treacherous grey cat since he was a kitten. It was hard to miss a cat that sprayed piglets and stole milk for fun.

Rupert's paws were tiny, his rib cage showed at all times, and his testicles were the size of walnuts. His ears flitted about as he looked up into the metal workings of the undercarriage. The mouse's tail flicked up into sight for a brief moment. Rupert tensed his shoulders and prepared to strike but his trance broke upon hearing John call for him. He lost interest in the mouse but made a mental note to come back later.

"Rupert? Rupert? Where are you? We're leaving. Come get your kibble. Here kitty, kitty, kit-ee!"

Rupert shot out from under the Jeep and rushed to his perch on the back window the main hut. "There you are, Rupert! How's my little kitty-kitty?"

Rupert sauntered up to John with a jerk of his crinkled tail. The two hideous testicles covered in fur were immediately apparent to Charlie and Joanna. Their stomachs turned when they saw the pumping blood vessels surrounding the testicles like awful netting used for collecting fruit.

Charlie and Joanna had their heavy backpacks on and were ready to head out. They divided their glances between John, who was feeding Rupert leftovers from breakfast into a metal tin and Arnold, who was clutching at his machete and glaring jealously at John. The air of the moment had a slightly erotic charge to it. Both Charlie and Joanna felt very anxious. It was apparent that Rupert belonged to Arnold. Arnold, in his simple mind, could not decide whether Rupert was being disloyal or John was purposely coming between the two of them. Both ideas maddened him. Rupert purred at the attention from both men and raised his shriveled anus in the air with sensuous gusto.

John turned from the little cat and put his gaze onto Charlie and Joanna. He was smiling.

"Alright, let's get out of here. Arnold, meet the fisherman when he comes and pay him double. Remind him that the meditation seminar is in two weeks. Think about going up to Ulako and getting us some battery packs. The LTS is running low. Gonna' miss you, big guy."

As the two aid workers headed out into the courtyard, John reached over to grab a red bandana from a shelf next to the doorway. He tied it around his forehead. Its contrast against the pleated khaki pants and burgundy collared shirt startled Joanna as she turned to make sure her mission leader was in tow. John gave her a wide, self-satisfied smile as he sensually brushed past her. He was beyond the main compound of the plantation when she noticed he wasn't carrying any weapons. Charlie began grumbling. Rupert had sprayed his backpack.

"We should be there in a couple days," John Rock said over his shoulder. "I'm definitely the most experienced hiker of the three of us. Three combat tours with Army Special Forces. What about you, Chuck?"

"Uhm...what?" said Charlie.

"Hah, yeah, thought so. Stick with me and I'll get you there. Mutobo won't even know what hit him."

From the stoop of the main hut, Arnold cradled his gray Rupert, who struggled to break the human's monolithic grip. Arnold's dim eyes watched as the rescue party departed. Where were they going? It didn't matter. The goats and pigs needed taking care of. He dropped the cat as an awful scent flew into his face. His meaty legs lumbered back to the corral where the goats were kept. Rupert scampered off in search of his mouse.

Chapter 4

An explosion rocked the rebel camp. Men flew from their posts and watched as their concealed radio tower plummeted to the jungle floor. They scanned the sky for attack helicopters. A second explosion rocked their mobile communications truck and it disintegrated into a thousand burning pieces. Long range communication was down.

"Lion, she is gone!" cried Young Johnny as he and Alistair ran up to the entrance of Walter's tent.

Mutobo spit out his cigar. "Unbelievable! Send everyone to look for her. She must be stopped and brought back here," he bellowed. "Walta', you round up the drivers and patrol the roads. Alistair, take three men and track her on foot. If you lose her, come back here and help us move camp. Johnny, you must leave for Pulai immediately and tell my family to go into hiding. Take Boy with you if you can find him. Let's hope he is still alive. If Ms. Wayne makes it back to her headquarters, she will retaliate against us. Careful as you track her, she will likely have more explosives. Stop in the villages and ask our patrons to be watchful. Tell them 'Mutobo promises a great reward for the white woman, alive'.. Ms. Wayne will bring her peacekeepers here if we cannot intercept her. Go, now! We will rally at Bura camp."

His jaws clenched and unclenched as he realized his massive blunder in not having his prisoner guarded more closely. Boy was known to spend too much time in the kitchen, joking with Alistair. The danger Ms. Wayne posed was immediate and deadly, she should have had two men guarding her at all times.

A young rebel ran up to Mutobo. "Sir! Sa-Sa is dead. He was in the armory. She stabbed him and took some explosives. There are no radios or rifles missing but she took his pistol, Sir."

Mutobo wiped his face with his hand and exhaled. Sa-Sa had only just joined the rebel group in the previous month.

"Bury him. When we are rid of Gemma Wayne you will go yourself to his mother with gold to pay for his funeral service. I need you to tell everyone in the armory we are moving camp to Bura." He gave the young man a solemn nod and went to the barracks. Later he would see what he could salvage from the communications truck. The time for direct action against the dam construction and its well-equipped UN guards had come.

Chapter 5

"What's that? Is that a GPS?" Charlie asked as he caught up to John.

An hour had passed since the rescue party had left the plantation and the walking had turned into light hiking. The jungle canopy was thick and the heat was slowly ratcheting up. The rescue party was on a wide trail featuring an assortment of hoof prints; a herding path used by distant villagers who traversed the mountain every few weeks to go to market. In his anxious thinking, Charlie had hoped to get to know John better in order to reassure himself that this was indeed the man for the job.

"What is that?"

"Hmm? What? Oh..." John took a pair of ancient headphones of from his ears and tinny, repetitive music could be heard. His face bore a confident smile. He adjusted his bandana up onto his forehead. "This? This is my Nintendo LTS. I'm playing Fizzle. Working on Robocyclix's 'Floating Ship' right now. Super tough stuff."

"What?"

"You've never played it? It's Fizzle. Nintendo bought the rights for it from Westfall Inc. last year. You know, Game of the Year for handhelds? Fizzle defuses bombs and trades them for coins. He's saving up for his own robot factory. Puzzles, adventure, and turn based combat all rolled into one? Come on. Even the kids in the Bura play it." With an incredulous look he put his headphones back on and continued walking on the trail, pausing only to pick a rock out of his sandal.

Charlie slowed his pace to fall back in step with Joanna. "He's playing a video game," he hissed to her. "A goddamn video game."

"Are you serious?" Joanna stopped in her tracks. "I thought he was guiding us with a GPS. He's been holding that thing out and muttering to himself for at least an hour."

"This is a complete waste of time. First, that weird-looking giant man. Then the cat, who sprayed my bag. And now this. He's playing video games."

"Let me talk to him." Joanna turned and trotted up the trail toward John. She tapped him on the shoulder as she overtook him.

"Hold on. One sec. Yes…oh, hi Joanne," Rock grinned.

Joanna's anger allowed her to steel herself. "It's Joanna. Mr. Rock, you're playing a video game."

"Yeah…what does it matter to you?"

"We're supposed to be on a rescue mission. You're a former Marine. This is unacceptable."

"You're not my Mom."

"What?!"

"You're not my Mom. I've done enough self-knowledge to know you're using emotional manipulation, in the moment, to get me to do what you want. I don't have to do what you tell me to do. You're not my C.O. either, so *butt out.*"

"Mr. Rock, I have no idea what the hell you're talking about!"

"You tried to tell me what to do and no one does that but my mom. Not even my C.O. told me what to do, especially after I had my philosophical awakening. Don't get your panties all in a twist cause I'm playing Fizzle. We're going the right way. There's a bridge up ahead. We still have a long ways to go and this is how I like to pass the time when I'm not in hostile territory. It helps me be more in the moment. Now please, Joanne, fall back and let me do the leading here. "

Joanna was speechless. John turned his attention back to the path, which was widening, took up his brisk pace again, and put his headphones back on. Charlie caught up to his fiancé.

"He says I'm not his mom. He said some stuff about an 'awakening'."

"Who the hell is this guy? Come on. Let's both talk to him." Charlie shrugged and motioned for them to catch up to Rock.

Their packs were heavy and it took them several minutes to overtake John once again. John was surprisingly nimble and sure footed as the path wound down to a bridge. Charlie and Joanna puffed and struggled and lamented having so much weight on their backs. The sound of a rushing river filled the air. Rock stopped dead in his tracks and bent down.

"John!" called Charlie, who was the first to catch up. "We're a little concerned that you're not taking this very seriously."

"Look guys, I saved my progress and put the LTS away. I won't play it when we're in hostile territory, which is actually just over this bridge. Look over there." He pointed to a support beam under the simple wooden bridge several meters away from them. On the beam was a small protrusion about the size of two fists. "See that? I put that there."

Charlie and Joanna crouched down to Rock's level and peered under the bridge.

"What is it?" asked Joanna.

John let out a chuckle, "I thought you'd never ask. It's a bomb. I was an Explosive Ordnance Disposal Specialist in the Marine Corps. Actually, it was more of a hobby that I got to use when I was forced to switch over to MP. I put that little sucker there in case any of Mutobo's scouts decided to come this way."

He turned his crouch in a swift motion of the balls of his feet and slipped in the mud, bracing his fall with one of his hands. "Ouch, ouchie. Damn." He picked at his hand before applying hand sanitizer to it from a small bottle he kept in his pants pocket. "Well, great, now my khakis are stained. Anyhoo, there's a little camera up there in that tree behind us." He pointed up to it and his companions followed his eyes. "It's solar-powered. Cool, huh? Got Arnie to climb up there and install it. We've got a bunch more scattered on the outskirts of the property. They're linked to our mainframe back at the compound. Set up all the hardware by myself.

Got a quad boot OS for gaming linked in, too. There are signal relay boosters all over this jungle for those little suckers." His gaze had returned back to Joanna's figure.

"What?" she asked.

"Oh, nothing, you just look pretty."

"John, you'll forgive us if we have some serious doubts about you being who you say you are. There's no way that's a bomb," said Charlie. "Mutobo is one of Zabon's most wanted men. There are posters of him up everywhere in Pulai. You were just playing video games. How do you expect us to take you seriously?"

"Fine, fine, need a little proof? Here's my tattoo for one." He unbuttoned his burgundy collared shirt and took it off to reveal a concave chest, neglected by the sun for many years. Underneath a scattering of silky brown hairs lay a military tattoo with several stars. "I told you that you needed to trust me no matter what. We have a little time..."

"No, John, we don't!" pleaded Joanna.

"Ahem," John cleared his throat. "It looks like we actually have a little bit of time and it sounds like you want me to prove I'm the real deal so sit there and watch the master do his thing. Hold this."

He handed his handheld game to Charlie and shot him another incredulous look. He proceeded to climb down the bridge, pausing only to firmly tie his burgundy collared shirt around his waist. Charlie and Joanna found a grassy patch on the embankment overlooking the river and sat down. John was careful to place his feet only where he could see a foothold and eventually had the bomb in his hands.

"Usually I have Arnie place these," he called out to his companions.

As soon as he returned with the bomb he set it down on the grass and began to methodically piece it apart. "This is the receiver. This is the optional timer. This is the detonator. These are just wires. This is the plastic explosive. And there we go, defused. Now, I'm going to piece it back together and detonate it. We'll have to radio in to Arnie cause he'll come running once he hears the blast back home. He doesn't do too well with explosions, always worrying."

Rock reassembled the bomb as swiftly as he had disassembled it. Charlie and Joanna watched him as he jumped from rock to rock to get out into the middle of the river. He set the plastic explosive down on the surface of a rock, fiddled with its components for a moment, and then hurried back to the bank as quickly as he could. "Fire in the hole!" he yelled. The river water exploded outwards and fragments of stone were thrown everywhere. A painful concussion rang through the ears of Joanna and Charlie. "Awesome!" screamed Rock but the scream barely registered in his companions' ears.

"Jesus," muttered Charlie from his place on the ground. He took his arm off of Joanna's back and wiped some mud from his cheeks. They looked up to see Rock was on a small, handheld shortwave radio.

"Sorcerer's Apprentice, come in? This is Arcane Master. Do you copy? Don't worry about Wisdom Bridge. Do you copy? Check the cams. We are not under attack. Just showing the young pups how you kick some serious ass, over." The shortwave radio yielded nothing but static for a brief moment before its battery pack failed.

A pair of men could be seen up on the far side of the bridge, undoubtedly drawn by the explosion. "Oh good, tribesmen from Ulako," said John. "Hello! Hi. Here, take this." He held out several pink bills to the men as he crossed the bridge. Their concern with the explosion dissipated as they saw the money. "Do you speak English?" Both men nodded. "Take this and stay here. My friend, you know him. He'll be coming this way in an hour. Tell him that John said I was just testing the C4. The password is 'Rupert'. He'll know what it means. Don't forget. Seriously, don't forget."

"You put a bom' in the riva'?" asked the taller of the two men.

"Yes, yes," said Rock with a wave of his hand. "You know Arnold? Big guy, about this tall? I send him to Ulako for battery packs. You know him.

Tell him I was just testing. There's nothing to worry about. Actually, could one of you go into town and have lunch ready for three people by the time we get there? You'll do it. Get some battery packs, too. Thanks." He handed several more pink bills to the smaller of the two men. This man took off in the direction of his village as though nothing were amiss. John turned back to the shell shocked couple, who had joined him now at the end of the bridge. "They know us in Ulako. Arnie goes there for battery packs. Sometimes he fetches gasoline in the winter when the mountain cools down. The high school kids there buy his mushrooms, those drug junkies. Clean myself, in case you were wondering, only a hard cider every now and then." He rubbed his hands together and put them out in front his face with an open-mouthed, enthusiastic smile.

"Joanne, you're carrying my Nintendo LTS the rest of the way since you seem to think you're my mommy. Chuck, you're in the back. Squad, let's move out. "

Joanna and Charlie exchanged bewildered looks. Charlie then handed the LTS to Joanna and motioned for her to go ahead. They fell into step, temporarily convinced of his abilities. Neither had seen an explosive substance before, let alone someone who could harness its power so nonchalantly. John led the group past the taller villager while untying his burgundy shirt from his waist and putting it back on. The stiff fabric felt comforting on his skin.

 In the distance, the remaining villager fidgeted with his newfound money. He glanced from the hole in the river to the strange white people as they walked away.

Chapter 6

The roar of the bomb detonation shook the air along the mountainside and its sound waves carried into the plantation. Little grey Rupert paused only momentarily to perk up his ears in the direction of John's handiwork before resuming the hunt. He had gone back to the Jeep in search of the mouse that had eluded him earlier. The mouse did not seem to be in the innards of the Jeep any longer but Rupert persisted. He could tell there weren't any scent trails leading away from the Jeep. This mouse was a stupid mouse and Rupert wanted the playful torture that preceded its death to be long lasting. It was no fun when his quarry was so vigorous that he couldn't entertain himself for long without risking a getaway. This mouse's choice to remain in the abandoned Jeep told him that he would likely be able to toy with it for hours if it so pleased him. This thought shivered up Rupert's coy little body and electrified the muscles of his jaws. He couldn't wait to show that mouse who was boss.

There came a sniffling sound from the undercarriage of the car. Such a sound is inaudible to human ears but to a cat with plenty of killing experience, the sound was deafening and orgasmic. Rupert was beside himself. He followed the movements of the mouse with delicate silence and the surest paws in the valley.

The mouse scurried along the metal workings of his habitat with a little flicker of tail here, a flash of whisker there. He soon became aware of the presence of that putrid plantation cat, the one who allowed himself to be rubbed by the fish gut covered hands of the lumbering oaf.

This Jeep was the mouse's home. Up until now, the only disturbance here had been the lumbering oaf's occasional foraging of old engine parts. The mouse froze in terror and then collected his thoughts. Rupert would murder him and then find his mate and his babies and devour them. He could not allow that to happen. He was not the spry field mouse he had once been. A nasty knee sprain the previous spring had relegated him to living a more tranquil life here in the cozy metal confines of the Jeep.

A sprint to the underbrush in order to divert this grey demon was out of the question. Should he fight? No, he couldn't hope to best this destroyer. The clever mouse was left with only one choice, but it was worth a shot.

Rupert watched as the mouse poked his head out of the deepest recess of the undercarriage, a place too isolated to strike. Rupert chattered effeminately in anticipation of a race for life or death into the brush. A confident but tiny little voice squeaked out, "Please, Sire, allow me to have a moment of your valuable time." Rupert's eyes twinkled with bloodlust. He remained still. The mouse continued, "Sir, I know you will strike me down with all of your most considerable skill. I only ask that you hear me out before ending my inconsequential life."

"Go on, darling," Rupert uttered.

"Sire, I am a simple mouse. I live a simple life. You have cornered me and I recognize your great skill. I was a fool not to leave this machine when I had the chance. I am older now and it took all of my failing strength to climb up here. Alas, I have seen you kill many birds and mice in the area. You have taken many of my friends and I know I am the next notch in what must be a highly decorated scratching post. I have also seen that, to my insignificant knowledge, you have no mate. I know of a beautiful female cat who lives on the other side of the village. She is a calico and could bear you many stout kittens. I don't think you could find her without my expert help. I would like to propose to you a meager deal, of sorts, knowing full well that my fate rests in your good graces. Spare my life and I will lead you to her."

The mouse knew that even if his proposition were accepted, the pair of cats would kill him once they were united. However, by leading Rupert far away from his mate and their little children, the mouse could ensure their escape to a safer haven.

Rupert considered the words of the mouse and then spoke, "Darling, you don't seem to understand me very well. I don't fancy the females, I want a strong tomcat to keep me company. Ooh, me-ow. If you found me a big, strong stud to cuddle, I would let you live."

Higgins hid his immediate astonishment, compartmentalizing it for another time. He needed all of his courage in this moment.

"Oh, I see. Sire, I don't mean to offend you but I mistook you for the heterosexual kind of cat."

"Why is that, my lovely?" purred Rupert.

"On account of your massive testicles is all, Sire. You have *the* largest testicles of any cat I have seen, this includes panthers. I may be a simple mouse but I have had the displeasure of happening upon the odd big cat cousin the in my forages through the jungle and yes, yours are larger. They frighten me. Are they sentient? Goodness me! My thought was that perhaps they assisted you in your hunting, given your prowess for the kill."

"Come on down now, I'm getting bored. Let's have our fun, shall we?"

"A thousand apologies Sire! I am prone to extravagant language from time to time as my ailments have left me with considerable time for the printed mouse word. What an oversight on my behalf, of course you possess an affinity for the male member of the *felis catus*. I knew this. I knew this all along. Let's forget the calico on the other side of the village, shall we? I do know of a certain tabby cat, homosexual in disposition, whose company I had the misfortune of sharing last spring. If you'll allow me to continue..." The mouse wiggled his nose and looked expectantly at the cat crouched a foot below him.

"Go on, Little One."

"Right, well, fortune be told this tomcat goes by the name of 'Wallace'. He was a strong a hunter as you are, no! Not quite as strong of a hunter but rippling with muscles and oozing copious amounts of vitality. In fact, he is in large part the reason I came to end my odysseys through our splendid jungle home. Wallace is ruffian and a braggart; methinks he is your type? He lives quite a ways away from here but I do indeed know some shortcuts..." He gave the grey cat another expectant look.

Rupert's tension eased and his crouch turned on its side into a splayed-out pose which eased the mouse's anxiety.

"Right, then. I can see this tidbit of information is of particular use to you. Shall I tell you more, Sire?"

"Ooh, please, yes tell me more. I like Wallace already." The mouse froze completely still and his eyes seemed to be looking somewhere far, far away.

"Mouse" growled Rupert, "speak up! Don't be a tease."

The mouse returned to his senses at the sound of Rupert's growl. "Doctor, my knee!" squeaked the mouse as a spasm jerked his leg. His eyes quickly shot back into focus and he continued on as though nothing had happened. "Tell you more, I shall!"

Rupert and his newfound friend carried on for several hours with the mouse doing the bulk of the talking. The little litter of mice hiding quietly in the empty wiper fluid reservoir listened closely but was eventually lulled to sleep by the tales of the voluminous patriarch. The mouse appealed to Rupert's loneliness and won him over with his great promises. By the end of the afternoon they had shaken paws and agreed to set out that evening - after the mouse had had a nap, of course.

Chapter 7

Thomas Chatterton didn't care about the finances for the dam project. The Zabonese government was taking a loan from the World Bank to fund its construction. What he did care about was getting some veal cutlet and scallops for lunch. This was a primitive part of the world and he couldn't wait to hop aboard his private chartered jet and leave back to New York as soon as he possibly could. The steak and onions placed in front of him were close, though one of the steaks looked slightly overcooked. His nose curled.

As acting CEO of General Utility, a largely ceremonial position, Mr. Chatterton maintained a schedule full of boardroom meetings such as the one he was presiding over currently. Last week he had been in Belgium and tomorrow he would be in Ecuador or some other place. Chatterton's short term memory was fading as he approached his late 70s but his appetite remained strong as ever.

Chatterton paused his gorging to wipe the sides of his rolling cheeks. Present at this meeting were the heads of the construction companies enlisted to build the dam, UN Commander Richard Sutherland and two of his underlings, Chatterton's own assistants, and the Accountant, a man whose presence was a complete mystery to everyone else. He was not accustomed to having lunch breaks with others but had refused to eat in any of the other rooms of the GU headquarters in Pulai as none of them featured a plump leather chair like the one he had stationed himself in. CEOs of his stature were permitted certain idiosyncrasies and Chatterton full well intended to avail himself of these permissions so long as they were his to be had.

He spied the heads of the construction companies as he dabbed and fussed. They were Brazilians. The Accountant seemed to be American. The lone Zabonese was the Governor of the Danta Valley. He had at first regarded this Governor as though he were a child. After spending many drunken nights gallivanting with the Governor at the Presidential Palace, Chatterton came to respect Fredericks as his equal. They were bedfellows in debauchery and had plenty of fun with the President's concubines. The mischief they had wrought the night before was quickly setting in now that his hunger was satiated. Never enough sleep for this ceremonial CEO.

Richard Sutherland rose gingerly from his seat and made his way to the front of the room. "Gentlemen, I understand it isn't customary to lunch in the same room. Let's please finish as our generous host Mr. Chatterton has a flight to catch later this afternoon. If you'll please forgive the inconvenience, I'd like to call your attention to some matters of Intel we've had come up since the Wayne kidnapping," spoke Commander Sutherland in a whine.

Retirement for this non-descript man lay a mere three months away. Sutherland had become more and more resigned to spend the rest of his 50s accepting the fact that his once-rising star had been completely snuffed out by the scandals that had rocked his career at his former post in Oceania. For his massive blunders, the United Nations Security Council had relegated him to the lowest rung of the UN Command ladder: West Africa.

"As you all know, we have had to disavow the activities of Ms. Gemma Wayne as our forces are here for peacekeeping purposes only. If the international were to find out the nature of her missions in support of the Bura Valley Dam Project, we would face all sorts of scrutiny and pressure from neighboring governments."

 He gave a labored look to Governor Fredericks that was meant to be a wink and then rose to stand in front of a white screen. Projected upon this white screen was a satellite image detailing the Bura Valley. Sutherland glanced at the corpulent Chatterton seated at the head of the large conference table spanning the length of the room and noticed his contemporary dozing. Sutherland coughed loudly and Chatterton brought his feeble gaze back into the room.

"This is the Bura Valley. We have our Peacekeepers stationed here, here, and here. Next, please."

One of the Commander's assistants complied and changed the image.

"These spots right here are heat registers from our thermal imaging that have no known correlation with settlements or Peacekeeper patrols in the area. This was two weeks ago. Previously we had chalked up the absence of open fighting in the Bura and the Danta to the peace accord headed by one 'Mutobo', first name unknown. He is also known as the "Lion". Next, please. This thermal map was taken yesterday. We believe that the terrorist groups opposing the Republic of Zabon have agreed to work in conjunction to undermine our efforts in ensuring that the building of the Bura Valley dam takes place. As we are not permitted by the Zabon-Bogro Treaty to enter into these areas outlined here, we have been unable to ascertain the nature of these heat registers. Our attempts to infiltrate the terrorist organizations have failed, as made obvious by the capture of Miss Gemma Wayne, and our aerial reconnaissance has discerned nothing of value from the thick jungle canopy."

"What the hell does this matter?" asked one of the Brazilian industrialists, a short and sinewy character.

"Next, please," Sutherland motioned to his assistant. "Right, Governor Fredericks and I have called this meeting today in order to detail to you the movements and activities of the terrorist groups and to avail you of our plans to increase security in the Bura Valley, introduce new clearance procedures for the construction site, and establish a curfew for the road network leading to the site."

The Brazilians grumbled but said nothing. They were making millions of renminbi and had withstood several such changes in recent months without too much fuss. They had, however, taken to complaining as much as they possibly could at these meetings in order to leave as soon as they could. Their jobs were secure; their Brazilian employees were some of the most industrious workers on the globe.

Thomas Chatterton fell deeper and deeper asleep. Drool had formed at the edge of his pink lips and was starting to roll down onto his undersized business suit. Governor Fredericks leaned over and flicked the heavy man's earlobe. Chatterton once again brought his head forward and rolled his eyes from the recesses of his brain back into reality. Fredericks smirked with a self-satisfied smile.

"This is our only known image of 'Mutobo', terrorist leader and self-proclaimed 'supporter of the People'," continued the erudite UN Commander. The image was of Walter. "This was Mutobo's registration photograph from his only known year in Zabonese public schools. Most of the education records were lost in the war. This photograph places him at about 17 years old. He is now believed to be in his early 30's. Next, please. We have retouched this image and age-enhanced it to give you an idea of what he looks like now. You may recognize the image from his bounty posters." The retouched image featured a grey beard and different eye color from the first image.

"Excuse me, but why does this matter? To us, we don't care about this man. We are not hiring any Zabonese for the work site. This doesn't matter!"

The second Brazilian industrialist was anxious to get back to his offices. Tens of thousands of pink currency bills were not enough to temper neither his budding stress levels nor the buzz of his cell phone in his pants pocket. Both Brazilians began to argue and complain to the UN Commander while stamping their hands on the table. The underlings of both Chatterton and Sutherland rushed into the fray from the edges of the boardroom to argue their own objections and grudges. The Accountant left the room to take a call. Governor Fredericks stroked the scruff of the stubble on his cheeks as he surveyed the scene. He leaned over, nudged Chatterton, and then produced a flask of whiskey from his suit jacket. The old walrus slid his coffee mug over to the Governor and watched with a sleepy smile as his coffee received an extra kick. The two older men toasted and leaned back to watched UN Commander Richard Sutherland fail miserably at commanding the room.

A slam of a door sliced through the raucous din of the meeting and there stood a ghost, Ms. Gemma Wayne, glaring at every man in the boardroom. The underlings who had so eagerly joined the fray now whimpered back to their corners. The Brazilians, Governor Fredericks, and Commander Sutherland all straightened their backs in anticipation of the verbal lashing they were about to receive. Only Thomas Chatterton remained untroubled, thanks in large part to the mildly acceptable meal and sharp whiskey now coursing through his partially clogged arteries. He made an attempt to rise and greet the disavowed Head Intelligence Officer but slumped back into his leather chair as soon as his fleshy legs bumped the conference table. She had shown some warmth toward him in their previous meetings but it had since gone cold.

"Save it," snapped Officer Wayne. She burst into mad laughter when she noticed the picture of Mutobo's second in command being projected onto the white screen. Commander Sutherland fidgeted and considered saying something before being mowed down by the sheer fire that was in his subordinate's eyes. "Do you know where I've been?" she began. "Of course you do. You disavowed me. You left me to rot."

"Officer Wayne…" trailed in Sutherland.

"I said, save it! While you all sit in these offices and have your fruity parties with the President and his ridiculous little entourage, we are doing the heavy lifting. I've been playing nurse in that god-forsaken hellhole of a hospital for two years and this is the loyalty you show me? All of your intel has come from either me or my men. Your satellites show you nothing and the terrorist factions know that. I have been quietly directing your little war in the Danta and the Bura so that you-" she pointed at Sutherland and then at the Accountant, who just walked back into the room "-can stuff your faces and keep your little pickles wet with Zabonese girls. I am in a room of children, absolute children. You left me out there! None of you were capable of coordinating some sort of rescue effort? Commander Sutherland, why were my men sent to patrol the Bogronian border three hours after my capture? "

"Officer Wayne…" Sutherland made one more attempt at saving face.

"Just shut up, Dick! I've been on base and know all about your petty power play. You owe me now, big time. I'm wasting away here. We're all wasting away here but I'm the only one who cares. I should have had my own Command Center in the Far East by now. Enough is enough. We're going on the offensive. I'm going to personally see to it that these Afro-fascists are dealt with severely and summarily. We're doing it my way

now. I'm handpicking a company of men. We'll start with arrests. I'll
interrogate them myself. Then I'm sending patrols to skirmish and draw
out the terrorist cells."

"What about Mutobo? Surely you can't expect to take his camp without
heavy casualties, given his fortifications," the Accountant asked as he
casually sipped from a mug of coffee. She turned to meet his gaze. He
stood aloof and impeccably dressed. A stack of manila folders lay
gripped in one hand and his lifeblood in the other. This was the one man
in the room whom Wayne's wrath did not faze.

"I'll go after his family. I'll hit him where it hurts," she snarled and
stormed out of the room, tearing down the white screen with a vicious
sweep of her arm as she left.

The Brazilians were clever and each took separate phone calls, leaving
the building and resuming their lives as competent construction tycoons.
Commander Sutherland, having been thoroughly humiliated by his
second in command, took to commiserating with the older gentlemen
and their whiskey. "Maybe she should be left to run things," he thought to
himself as he toasted his oncoming retirement. All of the underlings
remained in their corners. Chatterton's pawed at their digital tablets and
awaited the departure of their master. Sutherland's pecked away at
ancient laptops and eyed the digital tablets with envy. Even the UN had
become miserly compared to the energy corporations. Only the
Accountant was within his wits.

Chapter 8

Arnold gazed at his beloved goats in a simple reverie. He loved his goats. They reminded him of the sheep his family kept on the farm in eastern Washington State, though his Nigerian dwarf goats were much cleverer than those sheep had been. Pop had sold the sheep to help Arnold get enough money together to attend classes at Washington State University in Pullman. Arnold had been one of the nation's premier defensive linemen and was offered countless scholarships to countless college football programs. His rock-bottom SAT scores, GPA, and a police arrest for possession of a controlled substance completely derailed Arnold's fast track to on the field success. A young man once hailed for his incredible field vision, ruthlessness with opposing front lines, and explosiveness was now cast out as a football pariah. Mom and Pop kept him on the farm for another year and then sent him off to Pullman, warning him not to try out for the football team. The year of hard work helped Arnold get past the pain and embarrassment of his arrest.

Arnold forgot his parents' stern warning as soon as he was sized up by the young men in the university weight room. They introduced him to the football coach and he became a walk-on for the Cougars of the Pacific-9 Conference. He was held out of his freshman season until injuries to several linemen ahead of him on the depth chart brought him into action during the fifth game of the season. Arnold flourished and gained all Pac-9 honors as a 19 year old. His professors passed him with flying colors even though he spent the majority of his collegiate existence smoking marijuana, listening to "oldies", lifting weights, and having sex with young women far, far away from the confines of their classrooms. In an effort to retain its grip on the money making machine that was college sports, the National Collegiate Athletic Association had allowed university professors to openly acknowledge their dubious grading practices when it came to student athletes. This change in regulations allowed Arnold to make Honor Roll and further cemented his disinterest in self-improvement through study.

Washington State University's closure due to lack of funding in Arnold's second year of college football once again set him back. Arnold went back to living with his parents and working on the farm. However, this paled in comparison to the tragedy that would happen just after his 20th birthday.

This tragedy came in the form of a terrorist attack upon Yankee Stadium during a home game. An airliner hijacked by Islamic terrorists had been flown into a sea of unsuspecting Americans and the resulting explosions killed hundreds. Arnold watched the replays on the news with his parents from the comfort of their farmhouse. The massive horror of the attack reached the corners of his dimly lit mind and shook him into a desire for action. The resulting benefit concert by great American icons the next night drove him to tears. The words of the President upon his visit to Yankee Stadium two days after the attack lifted Arnold's spirits. He enlisted in the Army and answered the President's call to war against the Afro-Islamic-Capitalists in Western Africa.

The goats called to each other from their corrals. The midday heat was hitting the plantation and Arnold felt thirsty. He took a sip from his bottled water and wiped his massive forehead with his palm after untying his bandana. The soaking bandana found its way back to his head. One of the mothers nudged her kid to a water trough. Arnold shifted in his sweat. The small wooden chair beneath him creaked in agony.

Private John Macy was Private Arnold Colfax's first friend in the Army at Fort Sill. Arnold admired how his friend insisted everyone call him John "Rock". He liked the way John argued with anyone and everyone over everything. Arnold felt safe and comfortable with the steady meals he received during basic, but what he did not enjoy was the punishment piled onto him by his Master Sergeant for being John's friend. Through all the extra miles of running, hazing by their fellow soldiers, and excruciating hours spent cleaning floors, Arnold stuck by John. The two did so well together that they were able to fool their superiors into assigning them to Advanced Individual Training at Fort Bragg. They washed out within a week, mostly on account of John's continuing insistence he be called John "Rock" and were sent to Fort Leonard Wood to become Military Police. They finished their training and shipped out to Bogro, where they were assigned to help train the newly minted Bogro Police Force.

After attempting to resolve his continuing problems with Army officials over his name by legally changing it to "John Rock", John quickly rose to the rank of "Specialist" and claimed to have put to rest his insecurities over his name. Arnold quickly followed suit and made "Private First Class" in recognition of his outstanding work in guarding military detainees. Arnold especially liked being "First Class" in something and celebrated by smoking the first joint of marijuana he'd had since college in the backroom of a brothel near the Zabon-Bogro border. This celebration led to many more joints and soon Arnold was known off base for his tremendous drinking and willingness to smoke with anyone who gifted him a "j". All Specialist Rock could do was ride along in the revelry and occasionally sip a mixed drink and try to dance with the girls who shied from his advances.

Their partying had no place in the Army. They understood this and made sure to steer far away from bars and clubs frequented by their fellow soldiers. By going to seedier places, Arnold found his way to psychedelic mushrooms and John found within himself an intense apathy for the structure of life on-base. In a sense, things were going really well for the odd pair. They were gaining something from the locals that they'd never had before: social acceptance.

Both friends earned their highest distinction during their time in the Army when their prisoner transport came under enemy fire. PFC Colfax pulled three squad mates, including Specialist Rock, to safety and put down over ten enemy insurgents with only two hand grenades and a rusted "KA-BAR" combat knife. His heroism dispersed the attackers and allowed the convoy enough time to clear the road and rendezvous with backup. John earned a Purple Heart for the Zabonese bullet that found its way to his right butt cheek. Arnold earned a Distinguished Service Cross for saving the lives of his squad and displaying great courage under fire.

Arnold stirred from his thoughts again after noticing Rupert leaving the plantation grounds off in the far distance. He scratched the stubble of his chin and wondered why there was a mouse walking slowly just in front of his treasured cat. His thumb rubbed against the small bag of mushrooms mixed with marijuana buds tucked in his jeans pocket. He considered whether or not the mouse was a hallucination. He thought about the recent hallucinations he'd had while rolling himself a joint. Rupert ceased to exist in his mind and the herbal smoke brought him back to the event that led to his expulsion from the Army.

The trauma and shock from the terrible killings of the convoy attack were apparent in Arnold's demeanor in the subsequent days. Both he and Rock were granted a week's leave and they spent the entirety of it partying with their Bogronian friends. Arnold did the hard drugs, whittling away what little intelligence was left in his numb skull, and John looked on. John's frail body and uncomfortable advances upon any woman who made eye contact with him turned off even the most permissive of the prostitutes in the slum. Word of a medal ceremony for the Purple Heart and Distinguished Service Cross reached the hard-partiers and pulled them from their stupor back onto base.

The medal ceremony was a condensation of all the notable deeds of US Army soldiers in action during the past six months. Congress could no longer fund the military intervention in West Africa and so the Army was left with only a brief window of time in which to dispose with the formalities. Major American corporations were no longer supporting the conflict either. Troop pullout in the region had begun. The better-funded United Nations Security Council Army would be taking over ground operations and ensure both Zabon and Bogro transitioned to democracy. The perpetrators of the Yankee Stadium attack were killed in raids after firing upon the Navy SEALs fire teams sent to arrest them. Operation "Democracy For Africa Now!" was coming to an end. Army brass wanted to spend the last of their budget making sure their subordinates were treated to a grand ceremony in order to stave off any thoughts about the oncoming prospect of unemployment back in the States. John and Arnold went to this overblown ceremony severely hung over from their week of revelry and in no mood to leave West Africa.

After four months of shelling from the now-defunct Zabonese dictatorship, the only building left in Bogro's capital that was worth an award ceremony was a large boxing gym.

"Don't fuck this up. I'm on to you two peckerheads," were the words Lieutenant Carothers growled at his two MPs as they stepped onto raised platform where the ropes of a boxing ring had once stood.

"Why don't you make me?" hissed Specialist Rock. Arnold thought this was funny and chuckled for a moment until his aching head reminded him where they had been the night before.

"Your ass is grass," Carothers fired back. Rock stopped dead in his tracks and eyed the considerably larger man from head to toe.

"Oh, and you're the mower?"

"Get up there," the lieutenant growled one more time.

On the stage stood General Walter Diaz, four star general and overall Commander of the US ground forces in the Conflict. Beside him was Lieutenant General Sam Baker, a man fast-tracked for the directorship of the CIA. Arnold knew this because he had seen their faces a hundred times on the video screens in the mess hall back at Fort Leonard Wood. Diaz reminded him of a Mexican Santa Claus. Christmas was Arnold's favorite holiday and he had been a very good soldier this year.

"For his extreme gallantry and risk of life in combat with a tough and determined adversary, the United States Army does hereby award Private First Class Arnold Colfax the Distinguished Service Cross, one of our most esteemed recognitions for service to country," Lieutenant General Baker spoke into a microphone as General Diaz handed Arnold his medal. Arnold smiled like a child at his Mexican Santa Claus and turned his attention to his angry friend.

"For being wounded in action against the enemy and in the name of our Commander In Chief, the United States Army does hereby award," General Baker paused for a moment to smile and wink at Lieutenant Carothers who nodded in return, "Specialist John *Macy* the Purple Heart, our oldest military award and one worn proudly by thousands of members of our Armed Forces. Here you go, Son."

John Rock did not take the medal from General Diaz but instead ripped the microphone out of General Baker's hand. The room froze in stunned silence at this egregious break from decorum.

"I'm sorry, General Baker. I'm going to have to correct you there, sir. My name is, in fact, Specialist John *Rock*, like 'rock n' roll'. All you COs think you're hot shit with the name calling and the ordering around but I'm' sick of it. Actually, we're all kind of sick of it. Aren't we, fellas?" He scanned the ceremony attendees for a sympathetic look. He found none. Some of the younger men were standing, ready to intervene.

"Specialist Macy, I'll call you whatever-in-the-hell I want to. Now, hand that microphone back to me and go and put yourself in the custody of those MPs over there," said General Baker as he pointed across the makeshift stage. "You have no idea what kinda' shit storm you just kicked up for yourself, Son. Men, come arrest this-"

"You're not my dad and that's not my NAME!" Rock roared into the microphone before dropping it and punching Baker square on the nose.

The loud crunch of Baker's nose was drowned out by the squealing feedback of the sound system. The two men locked into combat as Arnold instinctively ran over to the top of the stairs that lead into the ring to block off the stream of soldiers attempting to aid their commander. His fury from the football and battle fields returned as he proceeded to crack ribs with his thunderous fists and fend off the batons of three Military Police. For Arnold, there was never a moment's doubt as to who had his loyalty. Best friends were forever.

Due to shoddy workmanship on the part of the gym owners, the boxing ring stood on a platform raised an absurd seven feet off the gym floor. Ground Commander Diaz tumbled from this height after being bouldered over by Rock and General Baker, locked in their death grip, and broke his ankle. His screams of pain snapped Baker and Rock from their tussle momentarily until Rock used the distraction to pull Baker's pistol from its holster. He put the pistol to its owner's head.

"Everyone back off!" The entire gym again froze in silence. "I know how to use this thing. Arnold, come on. Let's get out of here."

John and Arnold positioned themselves behind their hostage and slowly eased their way out of the boxing gym. Every weapon in the room was trained on the kidnappers. Baker, fearing for his life, barked at everyone in the room to stand down. The three made their way out the back of the gym as the other soldiers gave them a wide berth. John called out one last time before the big steel door slammed shut, "If any of you follow us, I'll blow his brains out." He mouthed, "No I won't" to Baker immediately thereafter.

The three disappeared into the back alleys of the city. Baker turned up two hours later, bound and gagged in a brothel with a sign hanging around his neck that said "Asshole". What ensued for the following week was the largest manhunt in the history of the United States Military since John Wilkes Booth shot President Abraham Lincoln. The manhunt turned up nothing. John and Arnold had endeared themselves with the locals to the point of deification. The Army pulled up shop and left empty-handed, leaving bounty posters for their AWOL soldiers. The posters were promptly pulled down everywhere but the embassy district. It didn't matter at all as John and Arnold slipped across the border to live in relative seclusion on a plantation in Zabon.

Arnold was smiling at the lucidity his hallucinogens brought him until a distant explosion echoed from the far side of the mountain. He scrambled from his chair and sprinted to the back room of John's hut. He arrived just in time to hear "kick some serious ass, over." After hailing John several times with no response, Arnold bounded out to his small room in the goat corral and tore a blue tarp off a row of rifles and other weapons. John was in major trouble and needed his help once again. He tightened his bandana, loaded himself with as much firepower as he could carry, and took off at a hard run. The effects from his joint moved away from his brain and into his body. Running felt very good.

Chapter 9

"I know, I know, it's very scary to leave your home and never know if you are coming back. You are a good girl and your tears will soon dry. Here," Young Johnny handed Mutobo's daughter a small chocolate, "your father knew you would miss him very much so he told me to give you this. He said it was your favorite. You are so precious to him."

"You are very precious, my sweet baby girl," cooed Aishe. "Your father told me himself, he is retiring from the movement later this year. Soon we will all be together again and he will stay for good. Sweetheart, we have to leave now. Can you let go of the bed and pack your things?"

Marla relented and gave Young Johnny a big hug around his legs. She was six years old and the most darling girl of her neighborhood. When Young Johnny had come, she had stubbornly clung to the aged frame of her tiny bed. She had cried and cried because "this was home". The thought of seeing her father again, the man who was so tender and gentle with her, supplicated her tears.

"Thank you, Marla," said Young Johnny as he caressed her braided hair. He had had a daughter of his own before war had broken out on the border with Bogro and seeped its way inland, leaving destroyed villages in its wake. He let himself feel that old love for a moment before getting on with what had to be done. "Boy, run to the market and get us something to eat for dinner. We'll take it with us to Mama Alistair's." Boy dashed from the small concrete apartment, eager to prove his worth on this very important mission of relocating Mutobo's wife and daughter.

Aishe and Young Johnny packed only the most prized of the family possessions: pictures, several dozen rounds of silver, and keepsakes from Mutobo's deceased mother. Living supplies would be found at Alistair's mother's house. She would be expecting them within the hour in her small shanty in a neighborhood even the Zabonese Army dare not enter. It was there that Aishe and Marla would adjust into a new life and wait until the end of the year when Mutobo was set to relinquish command to Walter. Then they would all leave Zabon and go to live with Aishe's distant relatives in Namibia, far away from the notoriety Mutobo had earned himself as a rebel leader in the fallout of the Zabon-Bogro War.

Aishe took short breaks to rest. She was several months pregnant with Mutobo's second child. Young Johnny ran his hand through his greying hair and paused to consider the young bride now holding her sweet daughter. He had once had a beautiful young bride and daughter. The memory filled him with sadness. His rough hands searched his vest for some relief. He stepped outside to smoke a cigarette and await Boy's return. Perhaps he should have told Boy to meet them at Mama Alistair's.

"**T**he barefoot running movement started about 50 years ago. I'm surprised you didn't know that, Chuck." John patted Charlie on the back as they trudged up the muddy trail to the village of Ulako. "Normally I wear my ultra-thin sandals for the rougher trails around the mountain. I showed the riverboat captain how to buy them online for me so now he brings me a pair every six months or so. He was really grateful for my help."

"Why are you barefoot now?" asked Charlie.

"I'm really glad you asked. It's simple, Chuck. Shoes with supports built into them for athletics weren't even invented until the later part of the last century. Until then, man walked with little arch support and virtually no sole in the bottom of his shoe. The athletic shoe was a huge marketing gimmick. Now that sports aren't relevant anymore, we don't need to hobble our feet in 'comfort' and 'support' we didn't need in the first place. Actually, I'm working on a new, unifying theory of ethics concerning the oncoming age of barefoot walking but I'm keeping that one under wraps. Someone would have to be pretty persuasive to get me to spill that secret." He looked at Joanna from the corner of his eye.

"But you're slowing us down. Can you please put your sandals back on?" asked Joanna.

Rock had been stepping on nettles and large pebbles lying all over the muddy trail and crying out in pain. There'd been several times he'd nearly stepped in animal manure and stopped the others in order to wash his feet with the water from their water bottles. He began to reek not of manure but of hand sanitizer.

"Whoa, Missy! I don't think you guys understand. Hiking barefoot is *preferable* to hiking with ultra-lights on. Even the ultra-lights hamper the ability of the muscles in your feet to retain their strength in some of those really hard-to-get areas. You're asking me to negate all of the careful work I've done in the past three years and I'm afraid I just can't do that. It's either the ultra-lights or my LTS."

"What?" asked Charlie.

"I can either put on my ultra-lights, like you guys want me to, or you can give me back my Nintendo LTS and I can play Fizzle. It will distract me from the trail; Self-knowledge."

"You're saying you want your video game back?"

"It's the best way I 'barefoot' without getting caught up on the trail. It's kind of like my Zen. When you're out on the trails, gaming is one of the best ways to lose track of the time. You get into the zone and you just go."

"Honey, give him his game."

The hour that followed went by without a word from John. True to his word, he was completely engrossed in his 'zone'. Joanna and Charlie felt a lot of relief. As they neared Ulako, John gave his handheld device back to Joanna without a word and slipped his specialty sandals back on. He jumped up and down in place to ensure their snug fit, buttoned the top button on his dress shirt, and adjusted his pants. They entered the village from the trail and marveled at the solar energy panels posted outside of every hut. Chickens clucked and pecked at the ground. Women tending to laundry looked up and smiled at the newcomers. Curiously, there were no children to be seen. Joanna and Charlie felt even more relief as they reentered civilization. Both secretly hoped John would be more pleasant outside of the isolation of the jungle.

A tall villager carefully approached the three hikers while they stood in the center of a small plaza. "My brotha' say you buy lunch from his ba'. Follo' me."

From their place at the wooden table and benches outside of a hut, the humanitarian aid workers could hear the laughter of children coming from a two-room school on the other side of a thicket of trees near the bar. The couple conferred quietly and decided to pay the school a visit to see if there was anyone that required medical attention. John nodded at them as they left and turned his attention back to the brothers who ran the bar. He was explaining to them the importance of dressing for the jobs they wanted, not the jobs they had. They listened intently between large swigs of beer and amused smiles.

Very few of the children turned out to have any ailments and those that did were generally just sick with a cold or suffering from small throat or nose infections. Living standards in Africa had risen considerably in the last several decades thanks to the energy, mining, and agriculture investments made on the continent by millions of immigrant Chinese. There were even some Sino-African children present at this school, a surprise to Charlie and Joana. They had not seen Chinese outside of Pulai in the few adventure treks they had done in the past two years. Outlying villages in the mountains such as these had been spared most of the effects the Zabon-Bogro War and the resulting United Nations interventions. Small oil wells built by joint Chinese-Zabonese ventures gave way to small buildings marked by small solar energy transformers. Ulako was yet too remote for paved roads to reach it but the village founders had plans to open construction on one in the next year. Hope brimmed in the eyes of the schoolchildren and these two white Americans with stylish backpacks were all the more evidence that the big, wide world would soon come.

Charlie led the children in a round of "Row Your Boat" as Joanna and the teacher looked on. A man carrying boxes of schoolbooks into the office paused to admire the fun before leaving quietly. Everyone giggled as the different groups of children stumbled into their rounds, one after the other. Joanna relaxed into a chair and let herself forget about the pressing ache in her chest that had gripped her since she watched Gemma be kidnapped. Charlie, too, relaxed considerably. This was the first time he had been in a classroom since his Bachelors in Childhood Education. The joy of the children was infectious. Soon they were on to a spirited "Old MacDonald".

John walked into the classroom and pandemonium broke out. The children swarmed him, poking at his running sandals and giggling at their odd colors. John took a deep breath and rolled his eyes into the back of his head. He closed them for a moment. When he opened them, a large smile came across his face, not unlike the smile he had given

Joanna when he told her she was pretty. The other adults in the room were surprised at his pleasant reaction to the sudden onrush of howling excitement.

"I love kids!" he shouted and crouched down to hug many of the students. They buzzed with excitement when he asked "Joanne" to give him his Nintendo LTS. He installed a recently obtained battery pack into it, switched it on, and fiddled with the settings for moment. There was a murmuring of curiosity and then renewed pandemonium when the LTS shot a blisteringly-bright image projection out into the air of the classroom. John spent rest of the afternoon gaming with the children and allowing them turns tinkering with the responsive holograms of Fizzle while the other adults stole away to take naps.

"Sweetie, wake up."

"What is it?"

"I want to talk about John."

"What about him?

"Jo, I don't think he is who he says he is."

"He took apart that bomb pretty quickly at the bridge."

"There's no way he was in the Marine Corps. Honey, you're as big as he is. He is obsessed with video games and apparently knows everything there is to know about barefoot running. Those just aren't things military guys are into. They're into cage fighting and drinking beer. You saw the way he was eyeing those guys back at the bar. He wouldn't even touch the stuff! Next he's going to be telling us he's a vegan or a feminist."

Joanne paused to think. "His friend Arnold at the plantation was massive. There's no way that guy *wasn't* in the Marine Corps. He had the same tattoo. Is it so farfetched to think maybe John slipped through somehow?"

"Come on, Jo. He's going to get us killed. I bet you he doesn't even know where Gemma actually is. He's probably just leading us on a wild goose chase cause he's lonely and wants someone to entertain him. Mutobo is a hardened criminal. The UN calls him a terrorist. Do we really expect John Rock to rescue Gemma from him?"

"He's our only shot. I know this is a little bit crazy but no one else is going to help us. If you have a better suggestion, I'm open to-"

"How about this for a suggestion?" John broke in from some brush into the shade of the tree where Charlie and Joanna had been laying. "How about not talking about people behind their backs?"

"Jesus, John! You scared us," yelped Charlie. "Why were you listening to us?"

"I can't believe you guys would talk about me behind my back! Charlie, I'm not surprised you would but Joanne how could you?"

"Look, John, we're just a little concerned with how things have been going," said Joanna. "We totally recognize what you did at the bridge and your tattoo, but…you know…you're just really different from what we expected."

"That doesn't give you the right to talk about me behind my back. Who gave you the right, huh? Don't tell me. You think your right came from God, right?"

Charlie and Joanna were silent.

"Bingo. I knew it! You guys think your right to talk behind my back came from God, plain and simple. We all know Blue Hospice is a Christian organization. You guys are religious nut jobs, aren't you? I've got news for you, *God doesn't exist.* There's no such thing as natural rights either."

"John, that's enough," Joanna said in a raised voice. "Until you butted into the conversation, we were talking about how we're not sure if we can rely on you."

"I'm just saying, your rights on this one didn't come from a god. I can prove it, Joanne."

"I'm a part of this, too" said Charlie.

"You don't have to prove yourself to us anymore. What you did at the bridge was really impressive. We were just having a conversation, one you weren't invited to."

"Correction, I was invited to it when *you guys* started talking about me. Please tell me you've read *Honest Communication.*"

Charlie and Joanna were silent again.

"You know, *Honest Communication: Openness in the Moment* by Luke Fitzgibbons? New York Times bestseller? I'm gonna' try and use it with Gemma if she and I get a good reading on her life sense."

"Once again, we have no idea what you're talking about. We should be finding Gemma, not hanging out here and talking about self-help books" said Charlie as he turned and walked off in frustration. Night was falling and he had better things to do in the village.

"Now's probably *not* the time but I'm definitely willing to dig into it with you guys," John called after Charlie. "I think it could really help you guys, especially you," he said to Joanne. "It really helped me connect to my inner child and become a better communicator. Why do you think my buddies back at the cantina were hanging onto every word I spoke? It's all about emotions."

"I'm going to see about Charlie. Maybe some other time, John." Joanna put her hand on John's arm for a moment, mostly to comfort her own self.

As Joanna departed, the village children found John and grabbed at him until he produced the LTS for them. He watched her walk away and considered the ways he could help her to gain more self-knowledge. The ground they had to cover that night before camp would give him plenty of time to reflect. He shook off the children and his thoughts to go get some last provisions.

Chapter 11

Arnold made it to the bridge, running as fast as he could, in less than an hour. He shook the cobwebs from his mind, bent over to catch his breath for several minutes, and then spoke some rudimentary English to the man who was waiting for him. He and the man were acquaintances on account of Arnold's supply runs to Ulako. The heavy ammunition belts, rifles, and massive knife layering Arnold's hulking made the villager very uneasy and his voice quivered as he relayed the message John had given him. Arnold was very disappointed. The itch to pull a trigger was creeping back into his life. Idle days tending to goats and pigs and his best friend were fun and all but unlike John, Arnie really missed the structure of the military. He'd done his best to create some structure for himself on the plantation but bowed time and time again to John's intellectually superior stance of lassez faire living. Video games, fresh fruit platters, fried fish, and meditative séances were all part of the "Rockin'" lifestyle Arnold was learning to live. Mushrooms were remaining vestige of the hard-partying days in college and the military. Anything else and Rock would get on his case.

Arnold twirled his hair and stared off into the distance. The villager backed away slowly and left for his home. Arnold didn't notice. Should he go find out what John and his friends were up to? Should he go home and break into the stash of champagne and party really hard while Mother Hen was out of the house? Where was Rupert going with that mouse? Arnold had many questions but lacked the ability to come up with any answers for himself.

He climbed up to the security camera and clicked it back on. He stayed up in the tree on one of the thicker branches and started to doze off. The rifles weighed heavy, so he slung them off his shoulders and leaned up against the trunk. Dreams came and went. He was fixing a milking machine on the farm. The cattle came through the chutes and up into the building. The freezing morning air was a sensation Arnie had not had in many years, it felt so reassuring. There was a harsh voice that startled him. He looked around and there was only a barn cat. It hissed at him and the fear snapped him awake. In front of him was a squad of UN soldiers who had come to investigate the explosion they had heard from their outpost.

"Hey buddy-"

"He's awake."

"Get out of the way, Sumner. Hey, you. Snap out of it. What are you doing here?"

Arnold could see the men had his rifles and one of his pistols. He did a quick mental check, without making a movement, for his hunting knife and his holstered snub-nosed revolver on his ankle. Both were there. This was only the second time he had encountered UN soldiers. The last time had been in Ulako when he had stolen away from the plantation to do some late night drinking at the Aubame bar.

"Did you hear what I said? What are you doing here?"

"Sir, I don't think he can talk. Look at him. He must be drunk or something."

"Let's bring him in for questioning. Sumner and Gutierrez, arrest this man. Get him up and take him down to camp. We'll keep him in the back of the APC till he comes to-"

Arnold sprung like a panther. He had been pretending to scratch his ankle when a revolver appeared in his hand out of nowhere. He drew up the revolver and blasted the squad leader through the face while at the same time, the massive hunting knife found its way into the ribs of the soldier who had woken him from his nap. The third solder managed to fire off a shot but it was errant, a knife through his neck swung the rifle into the air as it roared. The three soldiers who had been detached to check out the bridge came running to the aide of their fallen comrades. Arnold disappeared.

"Holy-fucking-hell! LT's face is gone, man."

"Roberts, get the fuck down from there and find some cover!"

A body swung down from a tree branch directly above the foolish soldier and gripped him by the shoulders. A sheet of metal the size of a small sword sliced in and then ripped out of the small of his back and he screamed in agony. The two remaining squad members opened their fully automatic fire at the dancing shadow, cutting down their fatally-wounded friend in the process. The panther curled up into the tree and pranced off into cover.

"Let's get out of here. This is too much heat," said the soldier with sunglasses. "Lay down suppressive fire and we'll wedge our way out of this."

A shot rang out from the bush and drilled through the hip of the soldier providing cover. Another shot exploded through his neck as he fell to the ground. He choked on the blood and was no more. The last UN soldier emptied his clip into the bush and screamed. "Fuck you!" As he reloaded, Arnold came sprinting out from cover and tackled the last of his prey. It was a glorious hit; it reminded him of the hit he laid on Gaines in the Arizona State game. The man struggled to try and grab his combat knife but Arnold pinned his weak arms to the ground. "Why?" was all the petrified body could utter.

"Arresting is kidnapping," said Arnold, as if he were repeating a hard-learned lesson out loud to himself.

"Are you going to let me go?"

Arnold stripped the man of all his weapons, his radio, and his pristine combat boots while keeping a revolver trained at his chest. He pulled the survivor up by his collar and set him onto his legs as if he were a toy soldier. He held out his new boots to the man but pulled them away when the toy soldier tried to grab at them. "Restitution," smiled Arnold.

He turned the man around to face the direction of his outpost and kicked him so that he would move forward. The soldier had walked a hundred meters before he realized there was no one behind him. He sat down and cried.

Chapter 12

The moon shone with a brilliant fervor over Rupert and his mouse guide. A light patter of rain tap danced across the jungle canopy and filled the otherwise quiet air of the night. An unspoken tension had developed between the two animals. Rupert eyed the mouse hungrily and the mouse continuously glanced over his shoulder to appease his nervous thoughts. The two paused only so that Rupert could groom himself in the reflection of a pool of water. They resumed their march and were soon nearing Wallace's home. Rupert couldn't wait to meet his potential suitor.

"Higgins, Sire. That's my name. Yes, you haven't asked me so I supposed it would be best I volunteered a short tidbit about myself. You know, to create within you some semblance of sympathy as a means of staving off my own demise. Positively blistering out here, isn't it?"

"Less talking, more walking."

"If you'd allow me just one more, I promise you it will be brief, moment of your time to make a humble suggestion…"

"Fine, what is it?"

"You'll have to forgive me, in my youth I was a dashing young field mouse: born and molded into a wandering provocateur of sorts by the breadth of many life experiences. I sullied the flowers of many a mouse brothel, climbed great trees to avoid capture by severe predators such as your eminence, and captured the leader of a band of barbarian rats who had terrorized a field of my cousins using only my wits and nimble paws.

Yet now, in my infirmity, I have fallen prey –pardon the wordplay- to the pressure of these many adventurous nights. Alas, my leg will permit me to bear my carriage no longer."

"Your leg hurts? Is it your knee?"

"Doctor, my knee!" Higgins exclaimed and was grabbed by some unseen force. His eyes widened and only his whiskers twitched. The pattering of the rain stopped and the two were left in relative silence for many seconds.

"Why are you doing that again? Come, Little One, I have no taste for silly games."

The color came back into the mouse's nose and he wriggled himself back into his limping walk. "A thousand apologies Sire! You ought not to worry about my moments of seizure. They are remnants of the revelry of my youth. Too much time spent in the cellar of that moonshine hut, I suppose. Back to the crux of our conversation, I propose you let me ride on your back for the time being so that I may recover my strength and deliver you to your vigorous beau in good spirits. In the interests of meeting your lowered cognitive capacities for the spoken word, may I ride on your back?"

"Hmmm," Rupert paused. He broke his composure momentarily to nibble an itch on his oversized testicles and scratch at his ribs. "I don't see why not but be gentle, Darling. I've kept myself thin for a good reason."

Higgins crawled up onto Rupert and smiled to himself knowingly. He was hatching a plan to rid himself of Rupert. There was no Wallace the Cat.

"Right then, we best be on our way. Lovely viewpoint you have up here. Whoa" cried Higgins as his ride took off in a fast trot. "You know, I have never ridden on the back of a predator before. If my dear mother could see me now! There is something that I have been wondering about you, Mr. Rupert of the Plantation. How is it that you came to identify yourself as a homosexual?"

Rupert spent the next several hours listening to Higgins speculate whether homosexuality was genetic or cultural in origin. Very little of what the mouse said made any sense to him.

Chapter 13

The drone of helicopters filled the sky. Runners sprinted from rebel safe house to rebel safe house, warning caretakers of incoming UN troops. Signalers poked their heads out from windows and got the message along by banging pots and pans. Young Johnny dropped his cigarette and hurried into the apartment to gather Aishe and Marla. He cursed himself for not sending Boy to Mama Alistair's. The rifle slung across his back suddenly felt very heavy. The oversights were piling on and the sense that he was no longer the roaring fighter he had once been filled his head. Young Johnny connected with his fear for the first time in many years.

"Come, Aishe, we must leave. The helicopters are here!" he said. Aishe and Marla grabbed their bags and followed his lead to the front door. Johnny leaned out to see if they were safe to leave and was met with the voice of a woman.

"Stay right there!"

She was one story below, in the courtyard of the apartment complex, and was flanked by three Blue Berets. The Berets were the meanest looking men he had ever seen, all scars and grim expressions. Johnny could see several more Blue Berets trickling into the courtyard as a transport helicopter zoomed overhead. He slammed the door shut and pushed a heavy wooden chair under the doorknob. There was no other sturdy furniture in the place.

"Please, get in the kitchen and stay down." He pointed to the kitchen in the center of the tiny apartment and Aishe and Marla quietly crawled away. Aishe held one hand over her daughter's back and suppressed her own sobs. Johnny pushed a meager mattress in front of a window. Just then, a firefight engulfed the apartment complex. He carefully sidled up to the window and peered out. Bullets hammered the wall of the apartment. Up on the rooftops were rebels. They were jumping out from cover to shoot at the UN soldiers down below. Young Johnny could see Boy signaling him to hold tight. He took one last glance downward. The woman leading the squad of men was nowhere to be seen. He trained his rifle on the front door and calmly stepped back toward the kitchen.

Something slammed against the door, a boot. Young Johnny let out a burst of fire and heard a body drop. The firefight outside was dimming, the intensity had dropped. A rifle butt crashed through a corner of the front window. Johnny closed his eyes and dropped his rifle in order to cover the eyes of the woman and child he had been sent to protect. A flash bang grenade exploded in the living room and then a smoke grenade filled the air with its contents. He sent Aishe and Marla into the back room and readied himself.

Bullets rained into the apartment like a torrential storm. The Blue Berets had decided not to take any prisoners for interrogation. Boy, pinned down by enemy fire, watched in horror as three UN soldiers unloaded their light machine guns into Mutobo's apartment. Each of them unpinned a grenade and ran for cover as the explosions rocked the apartment. Boy wept in a rage and slammed his fist on the roof tiles next to him. He was pulled away by a lieutenant of the neighborhood's street gang. Gemma Wayne had led a hit squad to kill Mutobo's family. Blood pooled around the corpses of three bodies in kitchen. Gemma stood over them, flicking her cigarette ashes and conferring with her soldiers. They were to spend the night conducting similar raids on the families of other insurgents.

Chapter 14

"Our radio capabilities still do not extend beyond 10 kilometers. Ms. Gemma Wayne is nowhere to be found. I want someone to tell me something useful, Walta'. At least Johnny will be here soon," boomed Mutobo. "You would have me wait patiently until the dam was fully built and our beautiful valley was flooded. This is what I am saying to you: we must send Renee on motorcycle to Dende."

"Listen, my brother, we can't spare Renee or the motorcycle for this. We need him for operations. If you want to order it, then let's be done with it. You are the leader here and no one is disputing your abilities. I am simply saying that if you want to begin attacks on the construction site today, we cannot spare a single motorcycle or a single man."

"I know you are right" Mutobo breathed a heavy sigh that shook away much of his worry. "Come, we have work to do."

Mutobo and Walter left their makeshift headquarters to survey their new camp. They had positioned themselves across the valley from the construction site of the Bura Valley Dam. Up until now, this location had been a rendezvous point for oil and food smugglers. Mutobo's grandfather had gifted him the location as part of a tract of land in his will. The land was made open in the past year to any rebel groups operating in the area, a fact not unnoticed by UN satellites. As soon as the displaced rebel group arrived to set up their new camp, several UN patrols passing through the area were ambushed and captured. Mutobo was abandoning his campaign of education in the villages in favor of open combat with UN forces and attacks on the construction site. UN air superiority was neutralized by the thick jungle canopy and the surface-to-air-missiles left buried at many former US Army bases.

"We are growing in numbers as their funding and support runs dry. I like what I am seeing," said Mutobo as he lit a cigar. His mood lightened considerably as he puffed. "Commander Sutherland is the oldest active commander in UNSCA, what a joke. Gemma Wayne's work in Iran was a farce. She should have been discharged. She is a good soldier but her missions have all been sloppy. She is no leader. Maybe she got sloppy with the President and his Ministers, ah? Maybe that's how she got her post!"

"I think she is smart, Lion. Even more than smart, she is deadly violent."

"A mouse to kill the lion, I know. Have a cigar, the sunrise is beautiful."

Walter took the cigar from his friend and commander. "Omar says he saw John Rock in Ulako last night with two Americans. He didn't see the Bear with them."

"Really? What was John doing there?"

"He said John was talking to the Aubame brothers about their clothes. Can you believe that?" Walter chuckled loudly. "Telling them they needed to hire him as their consultant, for what? Is he going to teach them how to scare away their wives? All that man does is play video games and send the Bear to get batteries and soda."

"It's good the big man wasn't there with him," said Mutobo. Both men puffed their cigars in an air of nostalgia. "He's not right anymore."

"No...too many drugs, there's too much violence in him."

"What about the Americans?"

"Omar saw them in Jenny's schoolhouse, that's all he said. They were playing with the children and singing songs."

"Mr. Rock doesn't leave the plantation for anyone."

"I know. It's strange. My best hypothesis is that they are paying him a lot of money to do something."

"The only thing he can do is build bombs and get the Bear to fight for him. No one will hire him for munitions work and the big man wasn't around. What could he be doing with them?"

"It could have something to do with Officer Wayne. Maybe they worked with her at the hospital. You didn't exactly hide your face, did you? They could be looking for their friend."

"They could be, but why John Rock?"

"I tell you: I have no clue, friend. Hey, Omar," Walter called out to their village liaison, who was unloading supplies from a donkey. "Come here for a moment. We are talking about John Rock and his friends. I was saying maybe they are looking for Officer Wayne. Maybe they hired him as a guide. What do you think?"

"It seems likely, Sir. He's one of the only white men around. He spoke all sorts of darkness before he bought the plantation. I don't know. Word gets around about crazy white men."

"That's good, Omar," said Mutobo. "Did you talk to the Americans when you distributed the school books?"

"I saw them but they were busy with the children. I left the books in Jenny's office. Do you need me to go back to Ulako, Boss?"

"No, that's all. When you are done unpacking, let everyone you see know that Walta' and I are leaving for a reconnaissance of the dam. "

Omar turned his attention back to the last of the supplies packed onto the exhausted donkey. Its legs were weak from traversing the muddy smuggler's trails leading up to the new camp. Mutobo and Walter left camp to hike to a cliff overlooking the dam. The hike was just another excuse to spend time talking with one another about the direction of their cause and the logistics of upcoming operations. The reality was that Mutobo and Walter had calmed considerably since the Americans left Zabon. The immense work of the last two years in gathering opposition to the dam project and the Zabonese government had been relatively free of bloodshed. Were it not for the looming dam in the Bura, a sense of peace was rising in the countryside. Mutobo shrugged off the peace that Walter alluded to. This Gemma Wayne had become more brazen in her tactics in the recent months, a fact he quickly reminded Walter of. The Tamil Bridge ambush had been bloody. He had seen cold hate in her eyes when he had faced her in his tent. She was a threat and she'd somehow been unleashed. Conversation turned to deeper subjects and the men stopped to rest at a spring before continuing up the slippery path to the vantage point.

"Tell me, Lion, what will you do after this bridge is destroyed and Gemma Wayne is reassigned?"

"I've told you many times, my brother. I'll take the girls and my newborn son and we will leave to Namibia. You want to come, don't you? That's why you keep bringing it up."

Walter cupped some water from the rocks below him into his hands and drank. He sat back up and smiled at his best friend.

"I have no one here but you and your family. Zabon is my home but there will always be danger for us. First it was Bogro, when we were children, and then again when we were young men. The Americans came and they hunted us until their money was gone. Now it is the UN and our own government. We used violence to achieve our means and we will never be safe because of the men we have killed. Maybe it is better far away from here. We can start over again."

"But who will be President when they hang Dahidi and his ministers?" laughed Mutobo.

"I don't think you are hearing me, Lion. I have *no one* but your family."

"You have the men. You will take my stead. Why are you so sentimental all of a sudden?"

"What I am saying is that you and your girls are my family."

"Thank you, Walta'. You are the uncle to my child and the brother to my wife. Those are very kind words from you."

"When you leave for Namibia, I will go with you. Wait. Just listen to me for a moment. I consider myself more than an uncle to your daughter. I feel like I am a second father to her-"

"That is very kind."

"-and your wife, she is more than just a sister to me. I love her, Mutobo. I want to join your family. I want to share your bed and watch Marla grow old. We can have sons and daughters together and we would never know who the father was. We could be fathers together. You are my blood brother. I don't want your manhood. I just want to share your family."

Mutobo was speechless. Sweat trickled down his head as the heat of the jungle set in. He picked a stick up from the ground and worked some dry mud from the sides of his boots. Walter held his breath in nervous anticipation. "You want my wife? You want my daughter?"

"I want to be in your family more than I am already. There's nothing here for me."

"Did you talk to Aishe about this?"

Walter shook his head, "No."

"Why do you want to be in my family for? We are proud black men. We take wives, many wives, and they birth us children. There are plenty of women out there for you, Walta'. Why do you want *my wife?*"

"She is a beautiful soul and your daughter is an angel. I have been there with them when you couldn't be. We could make a stronger family together, Mutobo. Two men, one woman: when you get tired of her, I can take care of her."

"You want to put your penis in *my wife?*"

"Don't think of it that way! I wouldn't penetrate her if you didn't want it, only when it was time to have another child."

"I can't believe I am going to ask you this," said Mutobo. "What in the hell do I benefit from this arrangement, ah?"

"I know you. You get tired of the girls. That's why you come out here for months at a time. You aren't the family man you think yourself to be. You want male companionship and to breathe free air in the jungle and on the savanna. Like I said before, with me in your family, I could take care of your daughter and your wife when you need to leave and be by yourself."

"And no touching manhoods?"

"It doesn't have to be that way. You have known me forever, I'm not gay. I would kiss a man if I was drunk but I'm not gay."

"You would kiss a man when you were drunk?"

"It's the time to be honest. Yes, I would and you would too."

Mutobo picked at the caked mud some more. He scratched at the back of his neck and shifted his weight onto his other hip. More than surprised, he felt intrigued. "I guess I would. I have always been firm and fair with my soldiers. If they were gay, I didn't care. That's why our troops are so happy, Walta'. We let them express themselves."

"Just like I am expressing myself to you, huh? What do you say? Can I be in your family?"

Mutobo reached his hand into his vest and pulled out a flask. "We need to drink. This is too difficult of a decision for me. You have made a very good case. I get tired of Marla and Aishe, it's true. The baby is on the way and it will be another person to take care of. Have a pull before it gets too hot." Walter and Mutobo traded swigs of the flask and sat quietly. They relaxed into laying positions and were soon puffing at cigars again. "Can I be really honest with you, Walta'?"

"By all means-"

"I'm feeling a little silly now, it's the whiskey. This fighting has been really hard on me."

"I'll bet it has."

"Sometimes I think I'm going to retire a poor man with nothing but memories of fighting and marching and sleeping in the dirt."

"I know how you feel."

"Thank you. It wouldn't be so bad, you know?"

"What wouldn't be so bad?"

"It wouldn't be so bad if you joined my family. We can't be gay though, we are brothers. We wouldn't share a bed."

"What do you think Aishe would say?"

"She is a strong woman but she feels lonely. I am emotionally distant sometimes, my brother. She picks up on this distance and feels sad. With two men in her life, men who love her equally, she will have more than enough companionship. I think she would say yes."

"Can I be even more honest with you?" said Walter.

"Yes, but first have another pull."

"Thank you. Lion, I can't get hard anymore with women."

"What?"

"I can't get hard. My penis is lazy. I went to the Aubame's last month with Alistair and I couldn't get hard."

"You've seen too much killing."

"It's not only that, we were in the same room together with the prostitutes. Alistair saw I couldn't get hard."

"So…"

"So he helped me."

"What?" Mutobo sat up and spilled cigar ashes onto his lap.

"He helped me."

"I thought you said you're not gay."

"I'm not gay, Lion, but Alistair helped me get hard. He used his hand."

"So you are gay!"

"No, it was only once. I got hard when I masturbated last week. I thought only about women."

"Is Alistair gay?"

"I don't think so." Walter passed the flask back to Mutobo. "He told me that if you do it once, it doesn't count."

"You believe that?"

"No, but it helped me to get over the embarrassment in the moment. I'm not gay, Mutobo. I'm as straight as a spear. If I was truly gay, I would tell you. I can tell you anything."

"You are very honest, that is my favorite of your virtues. What happened in the brothel is judgment free for me. I just thought that I knew you better. I was surprised but I can see how you would be very nervous to tell me. Aishe would appreciate your honesty as her second husband. Come here, man." He pulled Walter over for a hug. The hug lingered longer than both of them expected. When they pulled away from each other, Walter looked deep into Mutobo's eyes.

"You're a little drunk."

At that moment, Boy roared into view on a ramshackle motorcycle driven by the lieutenant who had pulled him to safety the night before. Mutobo and Walter sat up and sobered up immediately upon seeing Young Johnny wasn't with the newcomers. Mutobo tried to stand up but fainted when he saw the tears in Boy's eyes. His limp body landed directly on Walter's rock-hard erection. Walter passed out from the pain.

Chapter 15

There was a hop in Arnold's step as he ambled home to the plantation. Though killing gave him nightmares, knowing he had done the right thing always put him in a good mood. The satisfaction in knowing that these soldiers, who no doubt fancied themselves tough men, soiled themselves in fright was enough to hum a little tune and smile at the setting sun. There was enough time left in the night and nothing to do around the plantation, so Arnold decided he would go home quickly and get some cash. Not only would the whores at the Aubame bar taste delicious, there might be some more UN soldiers spoiling for a fight at the bridge. Some shooting and some screwing: the Independent Beast was coming unchained.

John had tried to train Arnolds "inner child" with his studied techniques. First, they had tried offering the Inner Child some ice cream after discovering that Arnold really loved ice cream. They sat with their legs crossed, on pillows, facing each other and tried to focus on channeling positive intentions to the child.

It did not work. John put Arnold under hypnosis, using a book he borrowed from a university professor in Pulai. The professor and John had had a quarrel the last time they had seen each other. John did not feel the need to return the book. With Arnold under hypnosis, a menacing and guttural voice began to emerge. John tried to prove to the voice that he was the master and it the apprentice. The voice called itself the "Independent Beast" and overrode any of John's suggestions. John eventually gave up on the hypnosis session and brought Arnold out from his reverie. He explained to his dazed apprentice all that had transpired, leaving out the voice's dominance of John.

At different times in their friendship when Arnold would show a sudden preference ill-suited for John's machinations, John would warn Arnold about the "Independent Beast". This would placate Arnold's mood and peace would return to the friends.

Chapter 16

Chatterton had missed his flight and was roused out of his bed by his underlings.

"Sir, there's an emergency meeting! Officer Gemma Wayne killed a bunch of civilians last night. Her men carried out night raids against all of the major insurgents and their families."

"Please, Sir. You have to come. Commander Sutherland is going to put her in detention and promote Colonel Wassman to replace her."

He rolled his large frame off of the bed and into some slippers. A short shower and stiff cup of black coffee later, he was out the door and in a limousine to General Utility headquarters. The lone thought motivating him to attend the meeting was that he could see Gemma one last time before he left to Chile or wherever it was that he was going. He had tried to masturbate the night before to a mental image of her but found that he couldn't visualize her breasts properly. This is what he told himself. What actually had caused his erectile dysfunction was the bottle of Spanish sherry he and Fredericks had polished off while watching an action movie together. The white grapes rolled around in his head while he shifted and wriggled in his bed, trying to conjure up enough blood flow for a blurry intelligence officer.

Chatterton's blood pressure rose considerably as he walked into a warzone. The board room was littered with torn dossiers and manila folders. Gemma towered over Sutherland, with a boot on his chest, and a pistol aimed at a military policeman from Fredericks' entourage. She was in the middle of screaming when he opened the door. The pistol whirled around for a moment and trained onto him before it whirled back around to the uniformed officer.

"You can't fucking stop me, Dick. I'm getting my goddamn acclaim on this one and bringing in Mutobo. We shredded his family to bits last night. It's us or him. As soon as he figures out what we did, he's sending his whole brigade after us."

"Jesus, okay Gemma. Fredericks, call your boy off. Gemma, please get your boot off me. I was only kidding."

"You weren't fucking kidding. You were going to take me in. I'm not going in. I don't know why I come to these ridiculous meetings anyhow. You're retiring, Dick. Get over yourself! You don't have any authority here and you know it. What's your pension? Three hundred and fifty 'k' a year plus what? Answer me, fucker."

"…plus dividends on all the…"

"That's right, plus dividends on all the projects the UN has overseen in the last 10 years. Okay, so give it a rest. I'm not fucking playing around, Dick. I'm in charge here. Go away. Go to wherever Tommie is going." She pointed the gun back at a blushing Chatterton before holstering it. "Now, get me a cappuccino and a fruit salad from the cafeteria."

Commander Sutherland slunk out of the room, clutching his shoulder. Chatterton left with him in hopes of avoiding any more of the woman who now held no sexual appeal for him. Only Governor Fredericks, the policeman, several lackeys belonging to Fredericks, and the Accountant remained. He had an amused look on his face.

"Do you need more funding, Ms. Wayne?"

Gemma turned slowly to face the Accountant. "You're a loud one," she said with a smirk. "I don't need more funding. I need Sutherland to retire. I need Mutobo to keel over and die. Most of all, I need my damn coffee and something to eat."

"It should interest you that there were a few allotments missing from last year's audit that have showed up recently."

"What do you mean?"

"There were two Black Hawks delivered to one of your hangars this morning. They were deployed in top secret exercises in Nigeria for the last 8 months."

Gemma sat down at the conference table and stroked her neck, popping it from side to side. Sutherland came back into the room with a coffee and a plastic cup filled with fruit. Beyond his figure standing in the doorway, Gemma could see Chatterton tucking his shirt into his tailored tweed pants.

"The food was –uh- never mind," muttered Sutherland.

"Thank you, Dickie," she purred with considerable pleasure. "Sit down. Did you know about the Black Hawks we received this morning?"

"You were the first to know, Ms. Wayne," interjected the Accountant. "It's obvious who is running things around here."

"That's more like it." Gemma smiled. She cracked her knuckles and remembered the broken fingers of a man she once tortured during her last post. He had screamed and screamed as she joked to her companions that he would have a tough time cracking his knuckles.

"Ms. Gemma, I must be leaving now. I have some last-minute errands to attend to before my flight," murmured Chatterton from the hallway.

"Again? Weren't you supposed to leave yesterday?"

"Yes, I was hoping to get a picture with you before I left."

"It will cost you three thousand dollars. I know you and Fredericks are perverts. We have all of your late nights with Solifa and her friends in a dossier. Three-k, take it or leave it."

"Well…okay. I guess that's fine," the older gentleman stammered. He rifled through his wallet. Governor Fredericks walked over to his friend and put several hundred dollars bills into the open wallet. "Thank you, Fredericks. Ms .Gemma, do you take renminbi?"

"That's fine. Come on with it. I'm about to relieve our dear Commander of his post and send him home."

Chatterton produced a small metal camera from his jacket pocket and handed it to Fredericks. They walked into the boardroom together.

Chatterton cleared his throat as he neared Gemma. She curled her nose momentarily before remembering the old man did still wield some power with Central Command. The wadded up bills felt dry in her hand.

"Thank you. I'll be on my way now," said Chatterton. Fredericks accompanied him out.

"Ms. Wayne, I'd like to be quite frank with you," began the Accountant. "You are a remorseless killing machine. You were selected for this assignment and put under the command of Sutherland here because of his disposition toward your aggressiveness. We couldn't just give you command outright as that would arouse suspicion."

Gemma furrowed her brow and sat down to her coffee.

"You are being given these attack choppers because you need to go out and do what you do best. Mutobo and the other rebel factions in the area are of little interest to us, but they play an integral part in a much larger scheme. You are here to destabilize the region. You are here to get the world's attention on General Utility. You are here to draw the Chinese into a conflict. By killing Mutobo, who is sold arms at a considerable discount by the Chinese, you will incite the other rebel factions into open warfare. You may even unite some of the factions across the border. The United Nations will have no choice but to escalate their involvement in the conflict in order to protect the interests of the international business community, General Utility. This will break the arms accords signed by the US and Chinese forces. Since China was ejected from the UN fifteen years ago, she has been spoiling for a fight. We're going to give her one."

"Why not meddle with Sino-Japanese relations?"

"We're here because of oil. Algeria, Syria, Yemen, and Iran were all for oil. Zabon and Bogro are no different. We simply can't steal the oil outright; we need to paint a narrative for the general public. The Chinese have entrenched themselves on this continent. Their free market solutions have been commendable but much to the expense of the European Union, the United States, and their international body, us. We need the public's sympathy for when we go in to save the great public works project our beneficent Security Council has sponsored. Ms. Wayne, you are our killing machine. We have put the bad man in front of you, now go kill him. Your country needs you," he finished with a slight drawl.

"I want to be paid double."

"Certainly, you'll get double. You will be required to sign a non-disclosure agreement upon leaving this building." He motioned to four men in black informs who appeared from the hallway outside the conference room. They stood at either side of Officer Wayne.

"Why me?"

"Because you enjoy the killing. Because you did fine work in Iran. But most importantly, because we know your lack of a conscience will keep you quiet once UN and US forces begin their airstrikes on Chinese bases in Bogro and Cameroon."

"I could use these soldiers," she motioned to the men in black uniforms. She did not notice that one of these men was an international celebrity.

"I thought you would say that," said the Accountant with a smile. "There are reports, as I'm sure you've heard, of a UN squad being ambushed and killed in action directly on one of Mutobo's known supply lines. You know what to do."

Chapter 17

After a long night of hiking and traversing the muddy path to the home of Wallace, Higgins and Rupert were exhausted. They took a nap together in the shelter of some abandoned car tires. The nap left them hungry. Rupert found himself a wounded finch and devoured its head. Higgins nervously cleaned himself as he watched the sight and then foraged in some garbage. He found the peelings of a sweet mango and soon forgot what he had just seen Rupert doing. After some time, they reconvened.

"Wallace should be just over that next hill."

"That's it? Usually you talk so much more."

"Heavens, me-oh-my! Where are my manners? I forget myself at times. Yes, your strapping young beau is over yonder hill. If my memory serves me correctly –which it sometimes does not- he should be on the roof of his master's hut. He will see you from the moment you crest the summit and lay eyes upon his domain. Frankly speaking, he may have already chosen a mate. Homosexual felines do seem to be a rarity in this area, especially ones who were born this way –such as yourself."

"Are you coming, Darling?" asked Rupert.

"Me? I'd prefer not to. I didn't know this was an option. You have me quite at a loss for words."

"It's not an option. I was trying to be polite."

"Well, then," said Higgins. "I have a request…"

"Yessss?" purred Rupert.

"As we are now leaving the jungle and reentering the domain of man, where there are no trees, I would like to request that I scurry along beneath the shade of your figure. The sun is quite taxing, in my old age. Surely you understand."

"That is fine. Let's go."

They left the large piles of trash in the ditch that had been dug by nearby villagers and walked briskly out into a field of short, waving grass. There was a light breeze in the air. Higgins began to hum. Rupert didn't like this and allowed his strides to become longer. This knocked his small belly against Higgins' head and the message was soon received. Higgins became quiet again. The hillside grew steeper and steeper and as they approached the top, Higgins began to speak.

"You know, Rupert. I've killed many cats."

Rupert was surprised at being addressed by his name. He thought the mouse was being cheeky.

"Do you want to know how I kill them?"

"Shut up, little mouse. We're almost there. I don't need extra stress. I just cleaned my coat."

"I lead them to slaughter. Something you haven't learned from your years on that ruddy little plantation of yours is that Chinese eat cats. If the Chinese don't get you, Wallace the Hawk will get you."

"Shut up, you little beast." Rupert rammed his leg into Higgins. "Stop trying to scare me."

A screech filled the air and both animals froze.

"Doctor?" whispered Higgins.

Another screech filled the air. Rupert scanned the sky and saw an enormous hawk barreling down upon him. He sprinted as fast he could but yelped out in pain when he felt Higgins dig his claws into his soft belly. Higgins was holding on as hard as he could. This only made Rupert sprint harder for the jungle canopy. Something had gone very wrong.

"How do you like that shit, motherfucker?!" yelled Higgins. "Get ready for lift off. I played you like a fool!"

Higgins had indeed played Rupert like a fool. While very well-read and well-traveled, Higgins' childhood was what developed him into the brilliant mastermind of survival he now was. He had spent most of his formative months living in an American Army base after his mother had stowed him away on a military cargo plane. She had hoped he would lead a better life in the healthier economic climate of Western Africa. The Deep South held little promise for such a gifted young mouse, especially the snake and spider infested swamps of Florida. On this base, Higgins was exposed to a wide variety of human culture, mainly through his viewings of Western movies from his hole-in-the-wall apartment in the movie theater. Through the study and reflection upon the work of noted 20th Century actor, Al Pacino, Higgins came to appreciate the Machiavellian character type. Films such as King Lear and The Godfather inspired Higgins to develop his acting skills in order to ensure his survival without a mother to guide him. These early experiences formed Higgins into an amoral wanderer capable of vanquishing anything that stood in his path to happiness, dogs and cats included.

"You tricked me! Let go!" screamed Rupert.

"Give me a second. I need to wait until the hawk gets you, then I'll let go."

Rupert darted this way and that but eventually it was no use. The hawk dove a second time and connected. It dug its talons deep into Rupert's back. Rupert let out a blood-curling scream and Higgins knew it was time to let go.

"Goodbye, asshole," called Higgins as Rupert was lifted away. He limped back to the jungle, curled up into an abandoned burrow beneath the roots of a tree, and slept for most of the day. The trip back to his wife and children would take a lot longer without a stupid, murderous cat to ride. He was happy to have outsmarted another predator but ready to retire to peace and comfort.

Chapter 18

Northwestern University had not imbued Charlie with the kind of critical thinking skills he needed in the face of such peculiar adversity. His parents had not prepared for any kind of life beyond the go-to-college-and-then-come-back-home-to-work-for-your-father life that was in front of him. The dim horizon in front of him broadened with the first wink he had sent to Joanna's online dating profile. A video of her building an orphanage in Ghana piqued his curiosity. Mainly, it was the sight of her backside in short, tan shorts that had aroused his interest but the altruism of her mission was a nice excuse. Within him existed a genuine desire for companionship and adventure but not the kind he was currently undergoing at the whines and whistles of John Rock.

This wasn't what Charlie had signed up for. He wanted to do his two years at the hospital, go back home for study in a Master's degree, and get some hefty scholarship money for all the adventures he and his fiancé had been on. They would buy a little house together and she would get a job at the hospital in his hometown. Gemma was supposed to fit into the plan. She was their best friend, a woman they had come to trust with their secrets and their hopes. She had not once made an improper advance on Charlie and Joanna had never mentioned any jealousy. There was something hidden about Gemma but Charlie never tried to pin his finger on it. She would leave on assignments to some of the smaller clinics lying outside of Pulai and be gone for days. When she'd come back her stress would be quite apparent, as would her willingness to drink and flirt with expats and locals when they were off shift together.

The drinking didn't bother Charlie. The flirting bothered him. He regarded her as her own independent woman. He just thought that the flirting didn't mesh with her confessions of never having had a boyfriend. Joanna encouraged the flirting in the hopes that Gemma would find a great friend that would fit her dreams of having a best friend couple. The two pairs could move back home and be the center of a compassionate community. Joanna also encouraged it because she thought Gemma to be a little too tom-boyish.

Currently, Charlie and Joanna were resting by the side of the trail to Mutobo's old camp. John had decided that he needed a bath and was swimming in a nearby pool of water. He had asked Joanna for some hair conditioner as he had forgotten his bottle of red wine vinegar at home; Homeopathic solutions were much preferable to industrialized solutions. She handed him a travel sized bottle of conditioner as Charlie looked on and rolled his eyes. The young couple breathed a sigh of relief at not having to deal with John for a little while.

"What if Mutobo killed Gemma?" asked Charlie.

"He wouldn't do that. He'll use her to barter for some medical supplies or something," responded Joanna.

"How do you know that?"

"I don't. I'm just guessing."

"I bet he killed her. They probably raped her. That's so awful."

"I don't want to think about that."

"Why did you give John your conditioner? That was really weird. He didn't just take it. He had to give that speech about homeopathic solutions. Sweetie, he really smells. He needs some actual soap."

Joanna chuckled. "I feel sorry for him. His only friends are Arnold and that skinny cat that sticks its butt in the air. I don't know, he just seems so desperate to get our approval."

"You think that giving him approval is going to make him calm down?"

"I don't think anything is going to calm him down. He's probably never had a girlfriend, poor guy."

"No, there's no chance."

"What?" Joanna put her hands on her hips.

"He's not going to get with Gemma. It's impossible! She's way too polished for him."

"I was just thinking-"

"Put it out of your head. It's not happening. Gemma is like a perfect '10'. John doesn't even register. John is like a 'Q'. He's not even in the same registry system."

"They're both socially awkward, just in opposite ways. Gemma is really stifled and uptight. She doesn't ever talk about what's really going on for her. John is way too open and everyone feels uncomfortable around him. Opposites attract."

Charlie looked at his watch. "It's already ten. John should have been back a little while ago. I'm seriously not even going to talk about John and Gemma getting together. It's not going to happen. She's fucking kidnapped right now."

"Something tells me Gemma is okay."

"What? Your 'woman's intuition'?"

"No, don't be a butt. I was just thinking about it during breakfast: Gemma didn't scream when Mutobo took her. She struggled to get something out of her bag until he slapped her. That was weird."

"She was probably in shock. Maybe she had pepper-spray or something?"

"Come on, Chuck. They had guns. It just seemed really weird."

"We should check on John, and no more talk of John and Gemma. It's not happening."

They walked toward where they thought John would be until Joanna stopped them. A quizzical look came over her face and she shifted her weight to one hip. She scrunched her nose up and looked at Charlie briefly before they continued down the ravine to the pool of water.

"Hey guys!" yelled John.

"Hey John," Joanna called out. Charlie was annoyed with her friendliness.

"I'm almost done. I was actually doing some Pilates and talking through some childhood trauma. My Inner Mother is being a real b- right now, if you know what I mean. A little Pilates always calms her down."

Charlie and Joanna froze in their tracks as soon as they rounded the bend and into sight of the swimming hole. John was completely naked and doing a headstand. His penis was a little skin cap nestled in a bed of hair. Joanna retched and Charlie pulled her back behind the bend in the path. John had not noticed them come into view and carried on while his companions struggled to regain their composure.

"Yeah, usually Luke Fitzgibbons really advocates for getting win-win negotiations going with your inner parents but I don't find that works for me. My methodology is an improvement on his in that I give the inner parent something that will soothe them so that they can stand out of my way and I can be freer to pursue virtue. This is a variation on the 'Control Balance' that I improved on by making it more of an outright headstand. It maintains the integrity of the spinal column while engaging the hip flexors the way the original Pilates exercise was meant to. Really, it's a testament to my training in engineering that I was able to make the necessary modifications. Hey? Are you guys listening?"

"Hey, John? Could you put some clothes on?"

"Oh! I didn't know you guys had seen me. Was my spine straight? I have a really hard time judging since we don't have mirrors on the plantation. I think it's bad for your self-image to have mirrors."

"John! Please put some clothes on. Joanna is here and we're ready to move out."

Charlie rubbed Joanna on her back and comforted her as she regained her composure. The sight of John's penis mortified her. Up until that moment, she had seen John as profoundly un-sexual. She had forced herself into feeling this way as a means of fogging from his offsetting moments of interest in her. This was the same fogging that pushed her toward thinking that one of her closest friends may have a potential romantic interest in John Rock. Joanna was a confused woman.

"Here's her conditioner back." John tossed up the small bottle which was now empty. "I had to use a bit extra since I noticed I was getting some split ends on my chest. Come on, C-Dubz. Tell me man-to-man: should I shave my chest? I read in Wenzel Shmechel's *Daily Runner* blog that chest hair is an important layer to keep between your running shirt and your skin in order to prevent chafing but then I read in *Seduction Guide* that chest hair is not in fashion this decade. Actually, maybe Joanne knows better. Hey Jo, did you see that Pilates pose I was in? What'd you think of my chest hair?"

Eventually they were back on the trail and all taking deep breaths: John for his inner mother, Charlie and Joanna because John was somehow even more unbearable than the day before. Charlie didn't show the empty conditioner bottle to his fiancé. He stuffed it down into his pocket, next to his passport fob, and hoped that somehow she would not ask about it. Joanna had considered the conditioner gone the moment she handed it over to John and was unconcerned. The rescue party was getting really close to the camp. The tone and volume of John's voice kept rising each time he pointed out an empty guard station.

John began to think of his mother and his childhood. His father had been largely absent from his life because of work commitments to Monberte, a multi-national debt-collection corporation. Mother, Julie, was a yogi working at a high-end resort in the city state of New Orleans when Mike, father, had met her. John used to hear the story from Mother about how they had written each other letters for several months after she had serviced him with body rubs and a happy ending. None of what Mother made sense because postal correspondence hadn't been popular for a hundred years and happy endings were families being together, not estranged.

John thought of when Mother had caught him playing house with several girls in the neighborhood. Thanks to some holograms he had watched, he had sorted out a complex system wherein the girls would serve as a harem. Their currency was not in sexual acts, something John was completely oblivious to until he watched Arnold have sex at a brothel, but in compliments. It pleased John to no end to be complimented, especially for his intellect. Mother watched for a moment as the girls would present themselves at his feet, one by one and give him a special compliment before going back to their chores. John was in deep negotiations with the Martians and couldn't be bothered for more than a simple glance and an acknowledging tilt of the head back toward the direction of where the chores needed to be done.

"John! What are you doing with those girls?" asked Julie.

"What does it look like, Mom? The Martians are pressing for more uranium stores in the new trade agreement but I'm not willing to budge."

The three boys who were playing the roles of the Martians bowed to John before turning to face Julie and walking backwards from her. They had dart guns slung across their backs and suspicious looks on their faces.

"Ma'am," called the leader of the Martians, "We're going to have to ask you to step away from Chancellor Slicer-Beyond and remove yourself from the Palace. If you do not comply with our orders, we will be forced to compel you with the full extent of our might."

They drew their gas powered rifles and loaded clips of foam darts into their places. Chancellor Slicer-Beyond cast a glare at his mother and shifted in the metal mesh chair he had 3D printed especially for his Palace in his backyard. Printing anything he wanted was easy for John as Father sent him a hefty sum to his bank account each month for "taking care of Mother."

"You heard what the Martians said, Mom. Go back in the house and get Lucia to make us some chicken roast or something. We're hungry, especially The Harem." He gave a wink to the head of The Harem.

"John, those girls are branded and can't be in this Section. You're not supposed to be playing with them. I don't want Security coming here," she whimpered, already defeated.

"I'll play with whom I please, Mother. Don't call me by that name. My name is Chancellor Slicer-Beyond."

"Your name is written in the World," bleated The Harem.

Julie wavered. She was usually a strict mother. She medicated with the yoga. It allowed her to get space from the usual coldness she felt for her son. Branded girls from another Section were a big problem for her, however, as she ran her yoga studio from home and needed to keep her licenses. Each license had cost her a month in child support. Mike had been getting less and less generous as Monberte had run into legislation in several economic regions that hampered its collection efforts. John couldn't just have these girls playing in broad daylight for the neighborhood patrol drones to scan.

"John-"

"Open fire!" screamed Chancellor Slicer-Beyond.

The Martian delegation peppered Mother with their darts. These were special darts, coated in a material that caused them to pop like firecrackers upon impact. Julie covered her face with her hands and screamed. A class of ten yoga students watched in silent horror from their uncomfortably held extended triangle poses. The Chancellor and his Harem giggled and pointed until Lucia, the assistant manager of the studio, came storming out of the large house with a stun pistol that fired oval bursts of sharp discomfort. She had just bought the defensive weapon as a measure against the apartment dwellers that lived on the way to the grocery dispensers. The Chancellor and his Harem fled into the club house while the Martians took up defensive positions. Lucia nicked one in the legs as he took cover.

"This is what you get, Mom!" yelled the Chancellor from his high tower. "You try to boss me around all the time and I'm tired of it. Commodus, aim for Lucia's face."

The Harem handed their Chancellor chicken eggs and he pelted the two women of his life with them. A couple concerned yoga students came through the sliding door into the yard. A Martian switched over to a stun pistol he had stolen from his parents and hammered the students as they stepped onto the patio. They were knocked cold.

"I'm running my Harem. I'm doing trade with the Martian delegation. You can't tell me what to do anymore. My games have become a reality! I am the Keeper of the Thunder. Bow down or you shall continue to be fired upon."

John Macy had finally broken his mother's will. She fell to her knees just as Lucia was knocked cold by a Martian stun pistol. From this point forward in John's remaining two years of high school, Julie would not raise her voice at her son nor order him to do anything he didn't want to do. Upon graduating from high school, John told his mom he had outgrown her. He entered engineering school but dropped out to join the military.

Walter and Mutobo were brought back to consciousness by the messengers. Mutobo carried on up the trail to the lookout as if nothing had happened. His whole world had come apart and he could not process it on any level. Walter accompanied him in silence after sending the messengers away with word that there would be an attack on the dam by the end of the day. The UN troops stationed at the dam would bear the wrath of the angry Lion. None were to be left alive and the dam would be demolished with all of the explosives available at camp.

The messengers did their job well. Thanks to the muddied paths being dried by the sizzling sun, they were able to reach the rebel main camp in a matter of minutes. Side camps and outposts were notified. Sympathetic villages were roused and readied. Boy even fired potshots from the back of the motorcycle at a UN patrol as they rounded into view for a moment. Anger burned in the Valley. Word was out that Mutobo's family had been murdered. The rebels knew that this was their shining day to bring justice to their land.

The Zabonese Regular Army was well aware of the night's previous raids and chose to do little to intervene in what was going to be a bloodbath. UN troops were expecting reprisals on their security points near Mutobo's old camp, thanks to Arnold's destruction of a squad, and so they were massing in the wrong place. They were awaiting Lieutenant Command Gemma Wayne's grand entrance into the old camp via her helicopters. She was going to arrest the Lion and take him back to Pulai. She had no idea the camp had completely moved.

Mutobo breathed slowly when he reached the lookout point. He put his arm around Walter for support. His head was heavy with the deepest pain and he nearly slumped again. Walter winced and covered his groin with his palm. They looked down at the dam and the several buildings dotting either side of the Bura River. Its waters were brown from the downpour the night before.

"We are going to take those on the far side," he said, pointing to a pair of warehouses with metal roofs. "Have Sa-Sa ready with the heavy machine gun."

"Brotha', Sa-Sa is dead. You know this. Are you sure you can do this?"

Mutobo went to sit down on the ground.

"No. Stand up, Lion. If you sit down, you will never get up again. Stay here with me. Can you do this?" asked Walter.

"I can do it. I can bear this pain until tomorrow. Then I am leaving. I will go to Windhoek and tell her family that she is dead. I will beg their forgiveness. Then, I will be nothing. The Lion will have one more battle with the Elephant and then he will be no more."

"I understand. I don't have any words, Mutobo. I'm so-"

"Don't. Not today. Today I must live as the Lion. Tomorrow I will let my heart die."

They stood apart as Mutobo straightened himself to his full height. He lit a cigar and handed one to his best friend. The smoke curled up through their nostrils and lingered in the humidity. There was no breeze and there were no birds in the trees around them. An ant crawled up Mutobo's leg. He clasped it gently between his thumb and his finger and brought it up to his face. He dropped the ant onto the smoldering end of his cigar and then continued to smoke. Walter pretended not to see.

Mutobo began to talk strategy, almost as if there was no one around him. Walter listened intently and made mental notes. He was going to have to plan the schematics back at base camp for all of the lieutenants to relay to their troops and the neighboring villagers who wanted to join in the attack. The pincer movement in the first wave and the feint that would draw the helicopters into the line of fire of the heavy guns were brilliant movements seemingly off the top of Mutobo's head. His instinct as a battle commander was sharpened to a murderous point. The Lion had saved his finest battle for last.

"Are we there yet?" asked Joanna. She was tired, dehydrated, and nearly ready to give up on Gemma.

"I was thinking. I've felt pretty distant from you guys today and I think I know why. It came to me in the middle of my Eagle pose: we're not living our values. We came together for a very good reason. We value friendships. You guys really value...*Gemma*," he said her name with a creeping lecherousness. "I really value my apprentice, Arnold. Oh yeah, and Rupert. We have more or less the same values. There's a distance between-"

"John," Charlie tried interrupting.

John simply raised his voice a little louder.

"There's a distance between us because we haven't been living our values. We really care about our friends, right?" He looked at Joanna.

"Sure."

This was just the prompting he needed. He stopped walking and presented Joanna with a little plastic wrapper filled with a paste.

"It's energy gel. The sun melted it a little. See how a friend can help?" he asked with expectant eyes.

"Thank you, John."

"I knew it! See, that's living our values. The distance that was growing was plain for all of us to see. A skill that *Honest Communications* teaches us is to recognize that distance, accept that it's there, and then work really hard to change it whether it wants to change or not. Well, I added that last part in. Obviously, Fitzgibbons has some work to do in his approach to epistemology."

"That doesn't make any sense," said Charlie.

"Look, man. I have more experience in building philosophical communities than you so just, you know, keep your conclusions to yourself. You can't just inflict me with your conclusions. I know the most about self-knowledge also. As I was saying, I recognized that we were coming apart. We were so close in Ulako, at the school. I knew that should be the standard for our relationships. We aren't just people that passive-aggressively use each other to fill our own needs, especially me. We're truth seekers and we need to come together in a bigger way to help Gemma. Gemma really needs us to manage this situation for her. Whether it's a shoulder to cry on for days and days about how she was wronged, someone to put a little fight in her and remind her of her dad and brother back home (hopefully that's me), or weather her fits of anger because we can provide that compassion: she deserves it. She's our friend and we're going to save her."

"That's really heartfelt, John," said Joanna. She touched him on the arm, having forgotten what happened the last time she did that. John's eyes rolled back into his head and he took a deep breath. Charlie regarded his fiancé nervously before speaking.

"Thank you for really looking out for Gemma. It's obvious that you really care. I'm sorry I've been distant. It's been so stressful to have to deal with this whole Gemma situation that I forget that we have some things in common. I mean, I used to really like gaming when I was younger."

"You game?" John asked in a bright voice.

"Sure, well, not since we came to Africa. Back home I used to have some friends that liked to come over and hologram tag with Jo and I."

"Wow! See, I never would have learned that about you if I hadn't opened up about my feelings to you guys. I'm really glad I did. Seriously, that's the power of *HCOM*. Fitzgibbons knows what he's talking about when it comes to vulnerability. You guys *have to* read this book."

Charlie and Joanna were confused as to how John could express his emotions and an instructional book in the same thought but were very welcoming of a different John. They had grown tired of his edginess and intellectualization. A more open and warm Mr. Rock would be better if they were able to bargain for Gemma's life and retrieve her from Mutobo. They could use all the openness and warmth they could get in this shell-shocked state they were in.

"I guess I'm willing to read some of it."

"Seriously? No, seriously? That's awesome, Joanna!"

"You said my name right-"

"I have pocket copies that I keep sewed in all my shirts. Burgundy shirt...that's the chapter on The State. You guys are going to love this! Rest assured, in time you're going to learn everything you need to know about the nature of the society that surrounds you."

John began to tear at his shirt with a small, metal hook he produced out of nowhere. Charlie felt inspired to try a new, gentler approach with John in communicating this was not the time to be studying a book. He had no idea whether or not it would work as he had only ever addressed Joanna this way.

"John, I'm sure that it's really important to you to teach us this book. Now's kinda' not the time to do this. Gemma really needs our help, right?"

"Gemma does need our help. What was I thinking? Thanks, Chuck. Good memory."

The metal hook went back to where it came from and the burgundy shirt was buttoned back up. Joanna breathed a sigh of relief. Charlie felt completely bewildered and began to wonder if this was how he should talk to John for the remainder of their time together. John finished his finicky handling of his personal effects and turned his attention back to his companions.

"Now that we're being completely honest, and we can talk about this during the last part of our hike, I thought I would mention that I don't think you two have the healthiest relationship. I mean, Chuck, when you walked out on the conversation last night on Joanna, I could see that hurt inner child in you. I'm absolutely convinced that there's a hurt little child in you and that I saw him walk away from his mother last night. This is the stuff we need to be talking about."

Charlie reverted to his non-Fitzgibbons communication.

"What the fuck, John? We're out here in the middle of the jungle. Our friend is no doubt being raped by huge black dudes. Huge fucking black dudes! We're trying to save her. You're the only person who would help us and you're trying to mediate my relationship with Joanna? Am I the only person that sees that this situation is completely inappropriate? Am I the only person that sees that you're a lunatic and probably won't help us get to Gemma? We're probably headed to some hippie convention at a commune and Mutobo is off a hundred miles from here getting his rocks off with our best friend!"

"That's the inner child I'm talking about," said John.

Joanna restrained her partner before he could lunge at John. John went into the headstand pose he had been in by the swimming hole.

"Pilates is also a fighting style. I pioneered it. I don't want to fight you, Charles, but I will restrain you if it comes down to it."

"Both of you cut it out," Joanna snapped. "I asked a simple question and I want it answered. How far until we get there?"

"That's not what you asked," murmured John from his inverted lips near the ground. "You asked, 'Are we there yet?' I have total certainty about that."

"Fine, are we there yet?" repeated Joanna.

John pulled himself out of his pose and into another pose. He whispered "Namaste" before relaxing into his standard standing stance: hands in his pockets with his chin raised slightly too high for physical comfort.

"I'm going to trust my instinct on this one. You guys aren't living your values. I can see that you're willing to do anything to distract me from the truth that I have seen in your relationship. Oh, I see the truth here and now I don't feel curiosity about your experiences. Sorry!"

Charlie restrained Joanna. John raised a hand and held it up as he continued to talk.

"I'm not going to fight a woman. I already won that battle with my own mother. Similarly, I have mastered my Inner Mother. It's getting really obvious to me that you two fill parental roles for me and that's why I chose you. I can see that I chose poorly. I'm going to go ahead, without you two, and find Gemma myself. Charlie, you really need to work on your anger and I'm sorry your father was so mean to you. You clearly haven't resolved this. Joanna, you're a passive woman who prefers isolation to enlightenment. I tried to help you but this has gone way too far."

Charlie and Joanna stormed off into the direction they had all come from. John continued to call out after them but stayed in his place. He took up another pose, a mix of yoga and Pilates that he had recently imparted to Arnold. It was the "Beast Tamer" pose.

"My real friends, Arnold and Rupert, know that I lost my way with you two and I know that they'll accept me back at the Plantation when I show up with Gemma. Unlike you guys, we'll get couple's therapy and come into our relationship with a firm commitment to living our values. Please don't follow me. It would be too pitiful and as Rand said, 'Pity is the worst thing to feel for your fellow man'!" he shouted to them as they shrunk away into nothingness. They needed to be shown that he had the moral high ground and there was nothing they could do about it.

With that, John trudged up the remaining trail to the fringes of Mutobo's old camp. He defused several landmines along the way and planned all the things he was going to do to show Charlie, Joanne, and Gemma his *real* value. Maybe he would start a show where he talked about the concepts of HCOM. People had to see that these ideas were important and *did* merit pausing important life events for. Thoughts of the various topics he could cover in the show whirled in his head. They were all things Luke Fitzgibbons had addressed in his body of work at one point or another. John felt pleased with his originality.

 At no point did he connect with the idea that maybe Joanna was simply asking him how much further they had to hike, that she was weary and thirsty and had not had a good night's sleep in a week. Such details would not dim his bright and rising star.

Chapter 21

Jason Christmas was brought in with three other black-ops agents to Western Africa on a special contract by General Utility. His squad was hired away from the South Australian Special Forces for the princely sum of 300 million renminbi. The Accountant wanted to see to it that if Gemma Wayne failed in her murderous tactics against the rebel leaders in Zabon, there would be a sure-fire backup plan in place. Christmas was not hired for his special abilities. He was hired for his star power.

Christmas knew Officer Wayne's temperament and it did not bother him. His father had inflicted the worst of beatings and tortures upon him on their cattle ranch in rural Western Australia. The beatings only ended when Christmas drugged his father, taped his fingers and arms to his waist, and tied him to the back of a horse he spooked during a cattle drive. This occurred when Christmas was 12. He never saw his father again. He went on to living in Sydney for a time but was relocated as a vagrant by a government program to Darwin, the mercenary capital of the Eastern Hemisphere.

Life was kinder to him in Darwin as he learned that his cunning and charm got him much further than the brute force his father had inflicted him with. He took a job as an apprentice chef with a restaurant. The clientele were migrant laborers and soldiers of fortune who took their working vacations in Darwin to get away from the Pacific War raging between the regional puppet governments of China and Japan. Aside from a pair of civil wars in Western Africa, this was the only armed conflict in the world for the previous 30 years. It was enough to get China formally ejected from the UN for its open insubordination of United Nations edicts.

Christmas was exposed to the life of wealth and adventure that mercenaries and mining laborers lived during these years and couldn't get enough for himself. He learned how to lie from Chinese merchants, how to fight from hardnosed Australians that ventured to join the War as 'advisors', how to cook from the Malaysian chefs who ranked above him, but, most importantly, he learned how to make his money from the

Doberman-sharp Canadian businessman who ran the camp. The businessman, Walter Rooney, allowed Christmas to sit in on meetings and work as an apprentice during monsoon season. The work involved resupplying the remaining neutral camps at the fringes of the War so they could withstand the harsh weather and continue to produce a profit. Christmas learned the power of personality from Walter Rooney and how it could drive profits in a world village dominated by narcissists.

These days, Christmas ran a successful worldwide company selling hologram training courses in espionage, heavy weapons, counter-espionage, hand to hand combat, and combat-readiness fitness. The last course of this list was his money making machine. With the help of Indian programmers, Christmas developed a fitness suit with a holographic heads-up display that would conform to a person's body and then move them like a puppet to perform the exercises in his courses: the Powersuit. This invention made him a billionaire several times over and put him on the main page of every main media site on the Internet at some point.

His 3D video blogs were educative, entertaining, personal, and at times, very bloody. The most streamed episode in his cloud was a Coca-Cola sponsored "Rampage" with a bulletproof, modified Powersuit. One lucky winner controlled his Powersuit from a stage in Times Square. Jason was placed in the middle of a Pacific War firefight raging in the streets of Manila. The controller earned himself a lifetime supply of Coca-Cola, monthly Apple products for life, and a maxed-out Food Card from the United States Government by registering 50 kills against the Chinese. The episode finished with him having protected group sex with a Japanese concubine and several Japanese commanders. This alone netted him several condom endorsements and an offer to develop a Sex Powersuit that would take all of the work out of the act.

Not to be outdone, the Chinese government put up a bid for a mansion in Hong Kong, two Bugatti Starfires, and 12% stake in LanWei Electronics, and the lucky winner would happily direct Jason's body to score 50 kills against the Japanese. The program was a massive success and many user-controlled movies echoed that success in the next year.

Christmas' worldwide patent on the Powersuit had governments, corporations, and international banks lining up to lease the technology for combat applications. The Chinese were already making cheap knockoffs of the Powersuit and faulty units were showing up in their revisionist films about World War II.

The owners of General Utility were deeply divided on what they wanted to see happen with Gemma Wayne. It was obvious that the UN wanted one of their own, Gemma, to get the acclaim for bringing down the Lion. This would yield them further contract work in Western Africa and possibly draw China into another conflict. Many of General Utility's owners and board members, Chatterton included, had no problem with drawing Chinese attention to Western Africa and seeing Gemma succeed in her tactics.

A minority thought it would be a better marketing strategy to include Jason Christmas and paint a narrative where the UN was brought to its knees by the Lion and his Chinese weapons suppliers. If General Utility was shown to the public as acting out of desperation in order to save the dam with some celebrity influence, it was presumed that they would attract much less negative attention from the Chinese government. Jason Christmas' sales were highest in East Asia as Chinese were notorious for their dismal exercise ethic. His Powersuit sales in China had reached a hundred million the year before.

Everything was going according to plan. His goal was to quietly eliminate Gemma Wayne during the final raid on Mutobo by manipulating footage to show that she had double-crossed General Utility. He would save the day using the Shenzhen Arms ScatterRifle and the Powersuit IV and then kill Mutobo himself after an intense interrogation. It worked to his distinct advantage that Gemma was oblivious to his celebrity status and treated his squad with open disdain. His producers back at Christmas Media in Darwin could chop this footage up into exactly what he needed to once again be an Internet hero.

"We're flying out in two hours to Mutobo's main base." Gemma Wayne gestured to a projection on a screen. "I want troop carriers to land here and here. I will set down in the officer's compound with Blackhawk A. Here's a little hint: their officers live in shitty little tents. Knock them down as I make the arrest. UN wants to see the arrest so I need six HUD helmets for myself, the pilot, and our new black ops friends."

Christmas was delighted to have another angle on the action. His Powersuit vision enhancement footage would look fantastic inter-spliced with the older codecs of the UN HUD helmets, a perfect chance to market one of the Powersuit features.

"I want Blue Beret Team A with the first troop carrier and Regular Squad C to land in the second. This is your chance to prove to me Sutherland was wrong for wanting you guys shit-canned, so don't mess it up. Regular Squad, we will drop you off after the raid near Ulako so you can investigate our Lone Gunman stories. Seven of you should be enough to figure out what the hell is going on down there."

"Aren't you expecting severe opposition?" asked Christmas. "You did just kill Mutobo's family, didn't you?"

Christmas braced himself for what could be a big pay day. The Times had shoehorned themselves into his General Utility contract at the last second for any exclusives on the smaller raids. He had maintained his exclusive on the Mutobo raid for Christmas Media so that he could use his eventual arrest of Mutobo to market the Powersuit IV and the ScatterRifle. In the interrogation he would ask Mutobo what he thought of the ScatterRifle and perhaps even have him wear the Powersuit IV before executing him.

"Excuse me. You're Black Ops. That means you're quiet. Shut up."

"Please?"

"What do you mean 'please'?" snapped Officer Wayne.

"I mean, 'Will you please tell me what happened last night'? I'd like to know on a personal level."

Gemma's brain short-circuited. This was the first time someone had approached her earnestly and openly in the past two years. Jason's assertiveness was immediately sexy to her. She forgot that there were 25 men all congregated around her, awaiting her instructions. She forgot about the hangar she was standing in and the four helicopters that were behind her.

Christmas had seen her type before: furiously explosive temper and the guts to back it up, all wrapped up in the guise of a beautiful female face. This was the same as the wife of Walter Rooney and she had always had a soft spot for her husband's little apprentice. She spent many a night opening up to Jason about her marriage issues and he learned that her big show of aggression was to protect a wounded person deep inside. He could see this wounded person in Gemma the moment he watched her in the boardroom asking for more money to get the job done. He could see that escalating aggression with her was useless, so he honeyed up to her.

Gemma touched her hand to her hair.

"A personal level? Yes, I suppose we did kill Mutobo's family last night in a raid, didn't we?"

"Yes!" an Asian voice screamed in Christmas' ear. He was momentarily distracted as the voice told him how much The Time offered for that little tidbit. His eyes refocused on Gemma.

"Thank you. I just wanted to understand what we're up against. Please, carry on. I really didn't mean to distract you."

Jason knew that Gemma knew he had no fear. Such was the insight of the billion-dollar celebrity. He marveled at how she could not immediately recognize him. All of the other soldiers had asked him for jobs or a letter of recommendation already.

Chapter 22

Higgins limped along the way he had come from, pausing to take a rest every little while. Pleasure coursed through him. More than pleasure, relief was present. He felt relieved that Rupert was gone. Rupert would have surely killed him after he had delivered the promised male companion. The era of mice being tricked by cats was coming to an end. No longer did the interactions between these two species match their violent and brutal forefathers. Mice were emerging. Science, in the form of genetic manipulation, was allowing mice to live longer and more conscientious lives.

Higgins' mother had escaped from a science laboratory somewhere between West Palm Beach and Boca Raton, Florida. Her hardiness and bravery in the face of insurmountable odds allowed her to make her way to a Naval base. In contrast to regular sea ports, Naval bases were one of the few places "mega-mice" were allowed to live in peace. They were seen as the next phase in biological warfare by the Pentagon. This changed as soon as the "War On Mice" began. Higgins was the only mega-mouse living on a North American military base to escape the mouse holocaust. He escaped because his mother was the first mouse to read English.

Escaped mice were common in the early months of their existence. They were very successful in spreading their seed. These genetically-enhanced rodents at first represented a "growing issue" in the mainstream media. As roving packs of hyper intelligent mice began to kill and maim common household pets, America fought back. Cat breeders made billions. The fiercer the cat breed, the higher the payout. Russian fox breeders made trillions. For a time, the mega-mice seemed to have been killed off. In reality, they were simply regrouping in the Southwestern Province (formerly New Mexico, Arizona, and Nevada).

Quarantines around the world were enacted as part of a global War On Mice. Mexico was hit the hardest but citizens responded by incorporating mice into the national diet. Mouse empanadas and "El Dia del Raton" were widely embraced in the culture alongside such values as the Virgin Mary and soccer. Canada saw a complete absence of "mega-mice", thanks in large part to the strict border policies all of the border towns and cities enacted in order to keep Americans out after the collapse of the dollar. Neither mice nor Americans were welcomed.

After her escape, Higgins' mother settled in to her nightly routine of calmly standing in line at the chow line in the cafeteria. She would gather food from a small dispenser under the main buffet tables and then be on her way. Executive Order #34 landed on the desk of the colonel she lived with shortly after she shared her quinoa and berry mix with her son. Terror overcame her when she flitted down to the desk to see what the latest order by the lame-duck President had been. She dashed to Higgins and gathered what little she could before disappearing with him into a hole in a wall. The colonel came into his quarters and breathed a heavy sigh as he read the order. He took his boot off and quietly inched over to the mouse perch he had fashioned for his companions. He ripped away the curtain that usually covered it and raised his arm back to smash. They were gone. He was glad.

A general alarm was sounded. All enlisted men were to shoot or stomp any mice on sight. There was a terrible slaughter. Higgins and his mother narrowly escaped the carnage by stowing away onto a transport truck that was headed to the base harbor.

"Sorry ma'am, there's only room for one more," said a grizzled mouse as he stepped in front of Higgins and his mother. They were on the underside of a platform that lead onto a large battleship. "It's either you or your boy."

"But this here is a battleship! There's gotta' be room on it for the both of us," cried Mama.

"I don't write the rules, ma'am. I just enforce em'."

"You gotta' let us both on! The soldiers are coming here next. We have to leave America together. I need ta' take care of my baby."

"Only one of youse is gettin' on! Who's it gonna' be?" growled the guard mouse. "If you can't decide, ya both stayin'"

"Mama, it's okay. I'm not afraid," said Higgins.

"Oh chlie," said Mama as she bent down to wipe a tear from Higgins' face. "You a real brave one. Mama's real proud of you. I love you, Higgie. With all of my blessed heart."

She returned her attention to the guard.

"How much is his fare?"

"2 grams of cheese or 3 grams of catnip. Whicheva' ya got, mamma."

She handed him the cheese from her rupsack and turned her attention back to Higgins.

"Higgie, you're going to Africa. Our forefathas is from there. I never told you this but, we didn't always used to be white mice. We were once proud, black mice and we lived in the heart of ancient civilization. Yore gonna need all your wits and cunning about you to fit in over there. Use your thinking' machine, right there, and never let anyone get in the way of your true joy. Yore Mama's gift in this world and I'm always gonna' think about you."

She nuzzled his head and groomed him gently. She was confident he would succeed. Deep in her heart, she was happy that he was leaving America and going to a better life. "Back to Africa" she thought. Pride swelled in her chest.

"Go on now, honey. Go find a strong, black mouse and make lots of mega babies. I'll be just fine here. You know Mama gets by"

"I love you, Mama."

"I know, Brown Suga'"

Higgins walked up the makeshift plank to the small opening in the battleship. The guard stepped in between mother and son and kept a firm look on his face. He was not a mega-mouse. He was a brute and would rape and kill Mother if she tried anything.

Higgins turned back to look at his mother one last time before disappearing into the battleship. In that moment, he vowed to himself that he would never be a victim of circumstance again. It was his 5 week birthday.

Chapter 23

Ulako was filled with some of the most ardent Mutobo supporters in Zabon. The Aubame brothers donated a large percentage of their profits to the education campaign Walter had devised. In exchange for this generous funding, Walter had turned a blind eye to the small leaflets advertising the brothel that the Aubames included in printing orders for the textbooks. Boy usually distributed the leaflets to his classmates. The attitudes and perceptions around prostitution were still very tender in the Danta. The valley had seen a heavy history of child soldiers and child prostitutes in past conflicts. Mutobo changed all of that. The villagers of Ulako were forever grateful.

The chatter of Afro-Sino children was usually the first thing villagers heard in Ulako. Chinese study ethic was ingrained in these children. It was a common sight to see them performing gymnastics and balancing exercises in the town square just as the sun was peeking into the valley. Arnold was awoken by the commotion.

He rolled out of the double wide cot he was in. A prostitute, the Aubame matron, pawed at him to come back to bed. He shook off her hand and poured himself a glass of water. His head was clear, a rare sensation. This changed the moment the matron produced a pipe and packed it with an herb.

"Hong Kongese" she said to him as he gently took the pipe from her.

The smoke filled him and he remembered the night before. It was a slow night for the brothel until Arnold showed up. He didn't say anything. He just laughed and laughed as he was handed tankard after tankard of beer. Then came the marijuana. An opium pipe made its rounds through the few other men in the brothel but Arnold passed it up. Opium made him sleep for days at a time. He wanted to be awake in the morning to go and see what John was up to. The all-too-normal college kids accompanying him aroused a lot of suspicion in Arnold.

Six women passed in and out of his private suite. They left exhausted and whooping to the others that "Arnie is feeling it tonight!" The house matron sidled into the suite, kissed Arnold passionately, and told him "this ride's free."

The gymnastics in the square turned into tai-chi and Arnold remembered John's Pilates. He crouched, leaned back, put his hands on the floor behind him, and arched his back. The matron giggled at his pose and kissed his hulking penis before walking out of the suite. She was off to make him breakfast, a tradition she upheld for the rare gorilla that brought her to climax.

Arnold ate his breakfast and set out on his hike to catch up to John and the kids. They couldn't be more than a few hours ahead of him. John *did* have his special shoes on that allowed him to outpace most people but Arnold was determined. He wanted to meet with them before the midday sun set everything on fire. The mud squished under his new boots and he smiled. The smile triggered in him the desire for some mushrooms so he dug into a pocket and ate a handful. Their taste was bitter. He stopped at the last shop on the way out of the village and bought a coffee to cover over the taste on his tongue. It worked like a charm.

A couple hours into his brisk, coffee and psychedelic fueled hike, Arnold stopped at a swimming hole to bathe. There was a magnificent boulder in the middle of the large pool. Usually there were rebels bathing and playing here with villager girls but none were in sight. In fact, Arnold had noticed there weren't rebels to be seen anywhere. He had overheard an American laborer in the brothel say that Mutobo had pulled up camp but the details were lost over the blare of the house sound. He thought nothing of it at the time but now it seemed much more relevant and immediate. The thought troubled him. He produced a THC-laced hard candy from his pocked and suckled it.

The boulder was flat with small grooves on the top, rounded on the sides, and had a small amount of moss that made a nap seem perfect. Arnold challenged the oncoming wave of sleepiness and stupor by launching into an intense workout. He performed movements and postures that the Afro-Sino children in the village square could only dream of. His chiseled frame pulsed with vitality. The blood flow forced the psychedelics in his system out of his brain and into his body. He remembered his glory days on the football field. The thought tickled him and he launched into burpees and finished with a handstand on the tips of his fingers. He lowered his body down and then up again with the nimbleness of a pouncing cat. "Rupert would approve of this one," he thought. The memory of Rupert leaving with that mouse, and the total disinterest of Rupert in his loving master, stopped Arnold's workout cold. He dove into the water to wash off the sweat and then sat with his legs crossed on the boulder.

Where had Rupert gone? John taught him that attachment was an illusion. If he felt sad he was supposed to sit with the sadness, in the moment, and notice it. He heaved a sigh, scratched at his considerable latissimus dorsi muscles, and tried to notice the sadness. It didn't work. He noticed the birds in the trees were singing in specific patterns and in time with one another. As he listened, he heard heavy breathing, stomping, and what sounded like bickering. He dressed himself and crept towards the sound.

The young college students were arguing with each other in the distance. Arnold closed the gap by sprinting up to them. Joanna screamed and Charlie instinctively stepped in front of her. They relaxed when they saw it was Arnold.

"John" he said to them.

"John? Fuck that guy!" said Charlie.

Arnold picked him up by the throat and changed his tone.

"John?"

"Okay...ugh. He's -up- ahead a while."

Charlie gasped as he tumbled to the ground. Arnold stood, lost in his thoughts. Joanna helped her fiancé back up to his feet and then angrily tapped Arnold on his chest. Arnold grabbed her by her backpack straps and lifted her into the air.

"Okay! I get it! We're not supposed to mess with you. Please, put me down," she moaned.

He set her down.

"John decided we were getting in his way. He said he was going to save Gemma himself from Mutobo. The last thing we heard was him screaming 'Rock Style!' He was pretty far off at that point," she said.

"Hmm," grunted Arnold. He pulled two hard candies from his psychedelic pocket and offered them to the pair. He pointed to his throat. They accepted, not knowing what was in them. A flicker of amusement came over his face as they put the candies in their mouths.

"Why don't you ever talk?" asked Charlie.

"Don't need to" was all he responded.

"We're going to catch up to John and pay whatever ransom Gemma has," said Joanna.

"No! We're not," retorted Charlie.

A hard silence came between the couple. Arnold remembered the time John gave him the "Silent as a Rock" treatment for sheering the goats instead of the sheep. This was sort of the same thing, it seemed.

Joanna giggled. "Your face isn't making noise!" she spurted.

"What? Whaddya say, Ms. No?"

"Oh my god! Charlie, I think we're stoned."

"Huhuh. Yeah. Huhuh. My tongue feels like the sun is walking over it. Like a treadmill."

"Arnold!" she happily patted the massive man on his chest. He raised her up again, ready to slap her across the face if she kept touching him. "Wee!" she cooed.

"We can't handle our shit, Jo. Please put her down?"

Arnold complied. Charlie was stunned and loosely made the connection back to how he had addressed John with kindness in his voice earlier. Maybe there really was something to that Fitzgibbons guy. The thought flitted away and was replaced by the urgency of his warm tongue.

"What were we talking about?" Joanna asked Arnold.

"He doesn't know. Man, my tongue feels like an orange. Is your tongue weird, too?"

"Were we talking about tongues? What?"

Whatever patience Arnold had the moment the THC came over Charlie and Joanna was gone. He took off on his brisk hike toward Mutobo's camp.

"Wait!" cried Joanna.

She took Charlie's hand and giggled as he licked it. Arnold stopped. He realized he had given them the "thumbprint" candies he was saving for himself and John for when they got back to the plantation. "Thumbprinters" were candies laced with tens of thousands of micrograms of pure lysergic acid. They were called "thumbprinters" because they stamped permanent changes onto a person's cognition. A "thumbprinter" turned a person into a ghost gliding the eons of galaxies in the universe. Egos melted into pools of popsicle water and reformed to become crystal sculptures made of "beyond". People who thumbprinted never quite came back from their experiences. A prominent figure in the psychedelic movement had once said that he died "a thousand deaths" during his experience. Arnold cursed himself. These candies had cost him several goats. If there was anything he learned in college, it was that a daytripper needed a caretaker while they visited the stars.

The choice was to stay with Joanna and Charlie, perhaps guide them back to the swimming hole, and let them ride out the trip for the rest of the day -or- he could go aid his best friend and make sure Mutobo didn't take yet another white hostage. He squirmed and unslung the rifles and ammunition belts from his back and watched Joanna and Charlie. They were holding the backs of their hands to each other's and smiling. He made a tough decision. He hid the weapons in the hollowed out trunk of a tree. He took the backpacks off of his daytrippers, made sure he had enough water and food to get them through the day, and slung the pair over each of his shoulders as if they were bags of air. He trudged up the path and wondered if Mutobo had any orange juice.

Joanna squealed "wee!" as they left their things behind. Charlie was dead silent, focused on his breathing with the entire genius of his emotional apparatus.

On their flight to Mutobo's camp, Jason Christmas and Gemma Wayne spoke little to each other. Jason was more focused on fine-tuning his Powersuit for the confrontation that was coming than he was on the beautiful, poised woman sitting across from him.

Gemma, on the other hand, seemed to glance at Jason every five seconds, trying to make eye contact with him. He had pierced her icy veneer with a few simple words. Not only were his dashing good looks and straightforward confidence a turn on for her, his fabulous wealth was also appealing. She had learned very quickly about him by asking around. Gemma's career arch was Commander of West Africa and no higher. She knew this. There still existed a glass ceiling for women in the armed forces: the more international the organization, the lower the ceiling. She could join a smaller body and have a larger degree of power but this did not appeal to her. She wanted to break the glass ceiling. A Powersuit could help her with this.

Her intentions with Jason were unclear to her. Part of her wanted to use him for his power, for his suit. Part of her wanted him to touch her, to show some sort of interest. She was not used to the sense of vulnerability that was coming over her. It was uncomfortable. She took out her frustrations with it by stepping up her nastiness toward the men under her command.

The Powersuit had nearly full charge. It glimmered even in the bright sun. Green veins of shimmering light traced its contours, from head to toe. Glowing triangles dotted each of Jason's knuckles. By tapping his pinky finger against his ring finger twice, he could shut down or turn on all of the lighting in the suit. He had removed all of the sponsor decals from their usual places because of his exclusive contract with the makers of the ScatterRifle. The usual fitness features of the suit were present but modified in order to support Jason's highly unpredictable body movement in the heat of battle. Leaps measuring ten feet up into the air and fifteen feet away from a standstill were possible for him. A Suit-assisted sprint could reach 40 miles an hour. Leaping and bounding could reach 95 miles an hour. Most bullets were rendered ineffective. Strength, however, was not assisted by the Suit; Jason had to rely on his superlative hand-to-hand skills if he was disarmed by an opponent.

"Drop us down there for a minute" Gemma said to the pilot.

"Yes, ma'am," said the pilot. He did not want to mess with the woman who had knocked off Sutherland from his perch.

"Tell the other pilots to take up a holding pattern. Climb another couple thousand feet."

Jason's jaw dropped as he watched his commanding officer stop during the middle of a crucial mission, the most crucial one of nearly the entire General Utility/United Nations joint operation, in order to go into a hospital to look for a pair of friends. She was risking RPG fire on her precious helicopters and delaying the eventual capture of the most dangerous man in the region. He followed her in. A voice with a heavy Mandarin accent chided him in his ear for not taking in his ScatterRifle.

"Who are you looking for?" Christmas asked.

"A couple of…friends," she said as she marched toward her old post. Christmas was surprised. He made sure to register the surprise in his emotion index for everyone who was tracking in the live stream.

"What are their names? Maybe I can help."

"You should be back at the- well- never mind," she said as she turned to face him.

His heads up display told him that her body was exhibiting signs of arousal. A ten second survey done by Christmas Media upon compiling this information showed Jason that his fans wanted him to pursue intercourse with her. "More condom money never hurt my fleet," he thought.

"Why are you just standing there and staring at me? Is your suit a little tight?"

"Sorry. I was just synchronizing with the ScatterRifle."

"Nice one!" yelled a viewer from Bangladesh in his Fan Cam. He switched it off.

"You sure you want to be in here?"

She was getting annoyed.

"Are you looking for Charlie and Joanna?" he asked.

"How the- is it your suit?"

"Yup. It does data sweeps that supercomputers from 30 years ago could only dream of."

Charlie and Joanna became instant celebrities. Maxwell and Gorman's Cancer Tablets was considering a purchase of the Blue Hospice Field Hospital within moments.

"What does it tell you about me?"

He tapped his pinky and feigned candidness as though the Powersuit IV were powered off.

"I don't need the Suit to tell me about you," he said with a smile.

She looked at his lips for moment before continuing on. The employees and patients marveled at "sweet" Gemma in her military regalia and the worldwide celebrity in-tow behind her. They had always thought she was just a cute volunteer who spent her weekends at expat bars and tourist sights.

Charlie and Joanna were nowhere to be found. Jason's Suit detected Gemma muttering under her breath. It caught the word "fuck" and the heat cells in his groin region rose in temperature. He had to tap his hip to disengage them. She checked the shift calendar on the wall in the break room. He could see that her friends had not been on duty for several days. An alarm went off in his left ear. Charlie was a rare "AB+" blood type. A note was made to offer Charlie significant money in exchange for blood and bone marrow samples. Shenzhen Arms was working on something top secret.

"Let's get out of here," Gemma grumbled. "It was really stupid to come here."

"Why?" he asked.

"What?"

"Why was it stupid to come here? You said these were your friends."

"You're not recording this are you?"

"Nope. I powered most of it off. Just you and me."

"They're the only friends I have. They're the only people who have cared about me. I'm not an ice queen, you know. I have feelings and needs. If people were just nice to me once in a while, they would see that I can warm up. I can have a laugh and cut loose with a drink or two. I'm not always a bitch."

"I'm really sorry. You can open up to me about these things. I'm not on contract with you guys for more than a week. You can tell me if this is forward of me but- would you like to have dinner with me sometime?"

Gemma turned her back to him. He could see her stifle a sob as she crossed her arms. She took a deep breath and seemed to compose herself. His emotion index was reading "sadness" and then "relief". This was some prime time drama. She turned to him with a determined look in her eyes. A kiss would net him an endorsement with an international chain of high-end jewelers.

"I can put in for some leave once Mutobo is captured. My friends will turn up. I'll tell them the truth and maybe we can all get out of here for a while." It was less of a request and more of a strong suggestion.

"Ms. Wayne, I like how you work."

"That's *Commander* Wayne to you, shit-bird. We're still on mission. Let's get out of here."

They dashed out of the hospital, all too aware of the critical mission time they had wasted on Wayne's emotional tangent. She shoved orderlies and a woman on crutches out of her way. Their pain was a relish to her. Jason made sure to capture plenty of images of himself training his ScatterRifle on the rooftops of Pulai down below as they flew out of the city. He smiled.

Chapter 25

The attack on the dam was over almost before it started.

Rebel RPGs hammered every vehicle on the site before UN soldiers were able to commandeer them. Mutobo and Walter benefitted immensely from a table tennis tournament organized by the station commander. He had contravened Gemma Wayne's orders that the dam was to stay on full alert in order to give his men some much-needed relaxation. Most of the soldiers and sub-contractors were in an oversized helicopter hangar when RPGs hammered the helicopters outside. Alistair's squad had reached the hangar's exits almost simultaneously and barricaded in the majority of the dam's forces. It was a rousing coup for the rebels.

"Never had I seen such a victory, Lion. No casualties, no retreats. Only Dawune was injured."

"Yes? How?"

"The poor cub tripped on an ammunition belt and twisted his ankle!"

Both men exploded into hearty laughter. They were standing together in the jungle overlooking the base entrance to the dam. As per their custom, Mutobo withdrew a victory cigar and they took turns puffing from it. "It's going to be hard fighting in there," motioned Walter to the entrance.

"I fucking wish we had Young Johnny for this. He was a snake in the grass with room to room procedures. Are you sure Abdul is ready? Something tells me he's not."

"Confidence, Lion. Confidence. We're almost there. He'll set the charges and we'll be done with the whole thing. They can't have more than fifteen armed guards in there. No shotguns. Intel says there's a weapons cache near the entrance. The first part will be the hardest."

"Then Abdul has no time to waste. Send his team in. Double their grenades before they leave. Give him this."

Mutobo handed Walter the shotgun off his back. He patted his friend on the shoulder and winked at him, letting him know that he could keep the victory cigar. Namibia was calling Mutobo's name. He would need to have another talk with Walter about their curious encounter earlier in the day. Such strangeness should not be left unaddressed, especially if they were going to be travel partners. It dawned on Mutobo that he had never traveled for more than a couple days at a time with Walter. What would it be like? He shook the thought off and refocused his attention to the hangar. The soldiers were trying to breach their own doors. Each time they made it out into the clear, they were cut down in droves by the transfixed rifles of the rebels beyond cover. Mutobo chuckled when he saw how poorly trained these men were. They certainly weren't men picked by Wayne herself. "Must be Sutherland's men," he thought as he jogged to where the heavy machine gun was stationed. There was no danger around him.

Abdul and his squad were pressed back and out of the dam entrance. Time was running up and reinforcements were bound to come within 10 minutes from Pulai. They had killed several guards in the dam but couldn't reach the cache before the defenders had stationed themselves in front of it. Abdul had taken a round in the thigh. His lieutenants dragged the corpse of a rebel private behind them.

"Jesus, Abdul. Tell me what happened!" gasped Walter as he turned his attention to the large, dark man.

"Sir, more than we thought in there. There must be 50 men. Reginald took a bullet in the chest. He's gone. He saved my life. They've shotties in there, Sir. Close quarters trained, definitely, definitely," Abdul clicked his tongue at the end of his report.

"That doesn't line up with Intel at all. Louis, did we bring those breaching shields that were in the back of the Mercedes truck?" Walter asked a man who had been observing the attack with him

"Yes Sir."

"Go get them. Now."

"Yes Sir."

Spotters radioed in to Mutobo to let him know that they had seen enemy troop carriers leaving a nearby outpost and helicopters taking off from main base in Pulai. The carriers were not a problem as the roads to the dam had been mined in the early morning in anticipation of the attack. The helicopters would pose a problem. It would be manageable unless Gemma Wayne was with them. Mutobo didn't want to wait to find out. He concentrated all available men on the dam entrance. They needed to reach the turbine hall before the helicopters arrived.

"Walter, what is Abdul's status on the breach?" he radioed on his headset from across the valley. They were at the narrowest point in the entire valley and could have possibly heard each other by yelling at the top of their lungs.

"Sir, Abdul has a slug in his leg and is being taken back to HQ. I'm going in myself with breaching shields. We brought up some tear gas and gas masks. 2 man teams. Second man will be infrared capable. We will smoke them out and gun them down. No more games."

"Good. Did you hear the spotters? No Blue Berets yet. We need to hurry."

"Understood, Sir. I put out the cigar. It waits for later."

"Careful in there."

The heavy machine gun was aimed at the hangar. Mutobo readied its handlers for possible incoming helicopters. His receiver exploded with chatter. Gemma Wayne had been spotted over Ulako, coming back from the old base. She had several helicopters with her, including a Black Hawk. They weren't headed for Pulai. A man in a Powersuit was spotted sitting next to her. Mutobo started barking orders as he sprinted to the dam entrance. Their time was very short.

Chapter 26

Most chartered flights for Thomas Chatterton came with friendly stewardesses, ones that would give him a massage if he needed. This one was different. He boarded his stout frame into the plane and was followed by Governor Fredericks, whom he had convinced to "come for a little flight." The champagne was free and if they were lucky, they could get a little extra out of the female staff. Neither of the men had any idea where the flight was headed. Their best guess was Chile but it really didn't matter.

"Welcome aboard, Sirs," chirped the stewardess. Her name badge said 'Ms. Clancy'.

"Thank you, Miss," chimed in Fredericks before his host could say anything. "Would you please show us to the drink bar?"

"Certainly," she replied and gently guided her drunken passengers to a pair of cushy recliners across from a lavish minibar.

Chatterton thumbed the camera sitting in his coat pocket. He was about to take it out and look at the picture he had of himself with the lovely military woman when he noticed the stewardess bending over to grab a pair of champagne glasses. He reached across the aisle and gave her a gentle pat on her skirt. She pretended not to notice and calmly walked off of the plane right before the airstair retracted into the hull of the jet.

"What in the world?" muttered Fredericks as he and his friend watched her flip them off from the tarmac.

Ms. Clancy was a radical feminist and one of the last of her kind. She had taken the airline stewardess job, with all its intensive training, in order to better understand the legacy and plight of her airborne sisters. This was her second year on the job. Her tell-all confessional was done and she simply didn't want to do the job anymore. It had served its purpose. She realized this when she woke up that morning. Chatterton's advance was the cherry on top of her angry cake that would show just how badly women were victimized in the industry. Chatterton and Fredericks looked on in bewilderment as she mouthed words at them. They didn't understand that she was speaking into a microphone attached to one of her earrings.

The jet took off and the two dignitaries helped themselves to their undignified carousing. They were surprised when no one admonished them for standing as they took off. Fredericks spilled his drink on his companion as he tripped and fell over. They both giggled like children.

"That woman was a strange one wasn't she?" said Fredericks.

"One of the weirdest broads I've encountered. She was muttering something at us. Did you see that?"

"I did, I did. What do you think, Tommie?"

"I haven't the faintest, Old Boy. What do you say? Shall we drink to her health?"

"You know, I've been slapped, scolded, entreated to stop, and even given a bit of play for doing what you just did but never has a woman walked out on me before. You have a way with these modern women. Tell me, would you like some coffee in your champagne?"

He playfully raised a pot of coffee from the minibar and dangled it in front of his friend's face. They giggled some more and settled into their recliners. Soon they were feeling airsick and much more willing to see if in fact there was another stewardess on the flight.
"Tommie?"

"Hmm-"

"Is there a ginger ale in your arm chair?"

"Nuh-uh."

"I'm going to check the front and see if there's an attendant who can help us."

"Yeah-" Chatterton burped uncomfortably and put his hand to his stomach.

The pilot stepped out from the cockpit and greeted Fredericks as he was poking around the work station usually reserved for attendants.

"Looks like it's just us," he beamed at Fredericks.

"Really? I must say, this sort of behavior on the part of a Zabonese woman would not be tolerated. I should have brought my assistant with me. There's really no one else on this flight? Where are we going?"

"I'm glad as hell she's gone. She was straight up with us but goddamn, she's always recording things to herself. Fancies herself an author. Fine by me. I won't stand in her way. I will say, I'm glad I only flew with her a few times. Has a bit o' reputation with us pilots. She's a good woman, no doubt. No doubt about that."

"I see. It's just us?"

"Yup. Just us."

"Well, where are we going?"

"I reckon we're going to Rome for a stopover. Then Captain Skip is hopping on. He'll be relieving me but no worries; I'll stay on board with you fellows. We're headed out to 'Oolan Bater' I'm Chip, by the way. Chip Whitley." The redheaded man extended his hand out to the Governor.

"Please to meet you. That's Thomas Chatterton back there, acting CEO of General Utility."

"Sure, yup."

"Can I ask for your help for a moment?"

"Fire away, partner."

"We're both feeling quite airsick and Tommie is in need of some ginger ale."

"I can do you one better, Chief. I was coming back here cause I heard you guys like to party. If you can keep a secret, so I don't lose my job, I can 'help a brother out' …if you catch my drift."

"I'm not sure what you mean. Who is going to fly the plane?"

"Nobody! Unless there's some turbulence, we pilots don't have to do a damn wink of work. GU has all the best equipment. Top of the line aircraft and all that. We guide em' in and guide em' out. That's it. Since Jane Austen stepped off our fine little craft here, I don't have to keep up any pretenses at all."

"Then you'll fit in with us quite well! We keep a straight face for all the other men in suits but behind closed doors, we're young at heart."

"And rather bawdy!" called Chatterton from the cabin.

"Right on, brothers. Here's that ginger ale. It's all free so rack up that bill. I set us at a lower cruising speed so we'd have plenty of time to kick back and relax. Mind if I come back there with y'all and have myself a little ginger ale?"

The three moved to a small conference table and settled into some nice conversation.

"You fellows ever heard of a soberin'-up pill?"

Fredericks unknotted his tie as he replied in the negative. Chatterton slurred something.

"Let me tell you fellows a story. I been with General Utility for six years now. Made more money than a Bildeburger, screwed more stewardesses than a Saudi prince, and flown more miles than a Jules Verne book. Before this, I was a laborer up in Alaska. Oil sands and all that. Oh yeah, here's a couple of those pills. Clear you right up. You can even drink it down with a whiskey, if that's your deal."

Their sobriety instantly returned to them. Something about the pilot captivated their interest. They appreciated his candidness and found him affable in a far-off but familiar way.

"I got these working up there. See, the man camps get pretty rough and tumble. Lots of guys drinking themselves silly, some to death. Our shifts were too long. Management started getting wise to this when the work started getting sloppy. The counseling didn't take. The specialists either got their asses kicked or some of the men tried screwing em'. Anyhow, it was all a mess and I'm rambling a bit. To be honest, I'm stoned off my own happiness most of the time. The pills. Yeah. Management worked with some biochemists. They matched the money they were losing from the lowered workmanship, put it into the research, and came out with these soberin'-up pills. Personally, I don't take em' cause like I said: I'm stoned off my own happiness on most days. What's there to trouble me? I fly a 150 million dollar plane with little oversight and live in a secluded bungalow in Sardinia when I'm not in in the air. It's a good life and I'm thankful."

"I see," said Chatterton with the clarity of a man who has had an epiphany. Fredericks smiled warmly and sunk more deeply into his chair.

"I'm going to split up a bottle of this stuff and gift half to each of you. Never mind what it's worth cause it ain't worth much. Take it as a token you can remember old Chip by when you're sitting in on those fancy meetings with all sorts of corporate fellows like yourself."

"That is very kind of you. In Zabon, we trade gifts. Please, take my wallet," said Fredericks as he emptied its contents onto the table. "It is handmade by artisans in the Bura. This particular one was made by the grandson of a friend. He built a scan-blocker into the spine."

"I'm tickled pink. Thank you."

"Chip, I'm going to see to it that GU gives you a raise and a more important position with us," said Chatterton. "I value honesty and too few people are honest with me nowadays. It's not like before, when I built this company from scratch. Everyone is a 'Yes Man'. That's not what I value but in my older age…I'm not as sharp as I once was. The honesty remains. I am who I am. Honest about my shortcomings, honest about the direction my company has veered off into, and honest about my drinking! We are cut from the same cloth."

Fredericks was surprised to hear so many words strung together and so coherently by his partner. He felt a renewed vigor toward life and an intense pleasure when he glanced down at the packet of sobering pills in his hand.

"That'll do just fine, Mr. Chatterton," replied Chip with a gentleman's nod. "We're well on our way to being friends! Since we're from the same mold and all that, I'm going to let you in on a little secret. Those pills don't have a lick of nothin' in them 'cept for some sugar and a little something to clear up your sinuses."

The two older men were stunned. They glanced at each other and then back to Chip.

"The Real Chip Whitley *did* work in the man camps and all that stuff about research actually happened. I'm not pulling your leg on any that. I even have some of those pills in a cleaned-out pomade tin I keep with me in my traveling bag. It's all true and you can trust me on those accounts. The pills I gave you were some every-day anti-histamines. What I *really* gave you was some human warmth and compassion. You two fellows go from meeting to meeting, never meeting anyone with any real human sense to them. I can see it in you. Other than each other, I'm the first *real* person you have talked to in years. I know what's going on in your mind, 'Who is this guy?' 'Where did he come from?' 'How does he know this about me?' Those are all fine questions and I'd like to answer them."

Chip went to the front of the plane and retrieved a platter of fruit and preserved meat. He set it down in front of his guests and continued.

"My real name is Chip Whitley. That's the honest truth. That's what you're gonna' get from me. I'm from Idaho. Moved to Alaska when I was eighteen and worked in the man camps for 8 years. Made myself enough money to afford the outlandish tuition General Utility charges for pilots cause I figured I needed to make that kind of financial investment in myself. See, I have major goals and I need money to achieve them. So, for the last six years I've been working for y'all, " –he nodded at Chatterton- "and doing my thing. I've kept a low profile because some of the things I say can really get a man fired, especially in the corporate world.

During those eight years of working in the man camps, I witnessed a lot of things. I saw how my peers destroyed their mental and emotional health in the name of money. I saw how these screwballs pissed away all that money on getting drunk, whoring in Barrow, and buying oversized trucks for bogging out on the tundra. I saw that my own original motives of simply making some cash and buying a home back in Idaho were small-minded and meager. I saw that I was going to end up like those guys. So I made a commitment to myself and decided to go about affecting some sort of change in the world. You can't leave the man camps when you're on contract. They'll track you down. You've got all those body enhancements for the cold, the heat, and the atmospheric pressure down in the mines that you're worth a small fortune to them. You stay for your whole work contract. Once you're signed, you're screwed."

The older gentlemen glanced at each other. Each saw the flickering visage of a younger man momentarily in the other's eyes. Chip commanded their attention.

"What did I do? I floundered about for the first couple years. I spent a lot of time alone, thinking. I missed home. I played a lot of holograms, trying to get out of my own head. It was troubling. Shit, I even lost hope for a couple months there and started doing the things everyone else was doing. But I got curious about owner of the corporation I was working for. Mr. Chatterton, it was your company. I knew my brain was big time. I knew I had a real bulldozer churning up there but I couldn't figure out how the hell to translate it into success in my job. I got to reading your early essays on management. Can I call you Tommie? You cued me into some real fantastic writers. They were brilliant thinkers and they taught me what I needed to know about self-esteem. I can see that you considered all of this a passing fancy, that's why you went on to lead the life that you have. I was different. I took this stuff seriously. That's when I began to grow. I began to change in the ways that felt right, intuitively speaking. That time I spent alone turned into absolute gold. I applied the reasoning I was learning with that piston powered brain of mine.

Mr. Fredericks, twenty years ago you were also a very different man. It blows me away how far gone you guys are. You were both writers and thinkers, looking to revolutionize business and government with radical egalitarianism. You came up against personal walls and drowned yourselves in drink. Now you don't remember. On some level, you two get along so well because you appeal to the honesty in each other but are partners in medicating that honesty away."

"How do you know all this?" said Fredericks, through watery tears.

"I may be wandering but I am not lost, Governor. Allow me to continue my story: I came out of the man-camps at the end of my eight years having written several books, filmed two documentaries, and with a small fortune which I have already mentioned. I have been sitting on all this and biding my time. I chose to be a pilot for GU for a very specific reason: the high pay and the near total lack of responsibility the job requires. This bodes very well for pursuing side projects, which I have been doin'.

You two have been lost in Western Africa, lost in your own sorrow for longer than you think. Tommie, you haven't made a single important decision for GU in over a decade. Since I've been with GU as a pilot, I've flown you to the continent at least 20 or 30 times. I have watched you slowly deteriorate over time and bit my tongue until I felt it was the right time. That time has come. Fredericks, you've weathered regime changes because you're absolutely harmless. You're compelled to each other because deep down, underneath all that shame that you pacify with a bottle full of rum, there still exists in each of you a noble spirit. Don't get me wrong, you're too far gone now to leave your twenty-odd years of fogging. You're not going to join me in what I have planned."

Chatterton and Fredricks exchanged disappointed glances.

"I am appealing to you for your abilities to cull together money. Tommie, your personal fortune is the size of a small national economy. And what you can do, Mr. Fredericks, by means of laundering that money through the Zabonese government to keep Tommie from being implicated in what I want to do is considerable as well. I have a life's Master Work and at this rate, I would need to work at GU for another 25 years before I had the money together to launch my plan. I'm asking for your monetary support as a means of honoring the young idealists you once were."

"Anything, please," said Chatterton, a hope rising in his chest.

"I need you to get ready… for those Asian masseuses that have been hiding out in the bathroom for the last hour waiting on you guys to sober up enough to have sex with them. Ladies!"

A flock of black-haired women emerged from the lavatory. They enveloped the two older gentlemen as music came over the intercom.

"You guys crack me up," laughed Chip as he put on a pair of aviator sunglasses. "GU pays me too much money to worry about making the world a better place. My Master Work was to get a job with you guys. Come on! These women aren't going to party themselves! The World Bank sends its compliments. Job well done in Zabon."

Chatterton and Fredricks breathed huge sighs of both bitterness and relief and then heartily accepted the mimosas that were poured down their throats. They visited Sardinia during their stopover in Italy and didn't leave for weeks. Chip Whitley had a special sort of intellect that kept them on a strange adventure until their health burned out. They spent several weeks in a Swiss hospital "recovering".

Chapter 27

There were no soldiers at the outskirts of the rebel camp. The ground was marked with the signs of recent bustling life. Footprints and tire prints were everywhere. Every single outpost that had once held a squad of rebels and a radio had been reduced to a toppled shack littered with trash. John entered the fenced area that had just recently been a Mutobo stronghold and saw only food scraps, a few bent tent poles, a burnt out and abandoned truck that had been demolitioned, and a few other odds and ends.

The place had been abandoned. John was pleased. Obviously, Mutobo had heard from the villagers in Ulako that the great white man from the plantation was coming. Mutobo must have done some research on John and seen that he was one of the United States Army's most hated men. He had run, like a coward, and didn't know this would just make his enemy's resolve that much stronger.

John set about sorting through the wreckage of the communications truck in order to try and find some clues on the whereabouts of his quarry. He ran his slender finger across some twisted metal and brought it to his lips. He tasted cordite and chuckled at the misuse of one of his favorite explosives.

There was nothing in the cab of the truck to be found. No papers, maps, or clues of any sort on where Mutobo could be holding Gemma. John was at a loss.

Part of the bench seat of the truck had not burnt in the fire of the explosion. He sat down on the cracked green leather and produced his Nintendo LTS from his pocket. This would give him time to think about what to do next. A boss battle with Fizzle's arch nemesis had been nagging at him since he had been able to get away from Charlie and Joanna. Fizzle's sidekick, Helper Dog, was an integral part of beating the boss and getting to the robot factory grounds. John thought of Arnold as he gazed down at Helper Dog's digital form.

John stayed frozen in his seat for the next two hours, playing his video game. He stopped when he realized that Charlie and Joanna would probably be catching up soon. He was going to need to convince them that he knew where to find Gemma. He fantasized about Gemma for another fifteen minutes when the drone of a half dozen helicopters filled the sky.

Four of the helicopters began to land in the middle of the abandoned camp. John put away his LTS and walked toward the foremost of the helicopters. A short, athletic woman with a pixie haircut stepped out of the helicopter that John had been walking toward. His immense sexual arousal turned to iron anticipation as she pointed her men to him as he approached. Two men wearing all black uniforms approached John cautiously and then grabbed him by the shoulders. John struggled momentarily but was subdued by a punch to the gut. As he was brought to the woman, Jason Christmas, the world celebrity, stepped from the helicopter wearing one of his famous Powersuits.

John made it a point to be the first to talk.

"Who are you and where's Mutobo?"

"Identify yourself and your reason for being here or we will shoot you and leave you for dead," Gemma growled at John.

"Whoa, Missy! Calm down. I'm not the kind of guy you want to fuck with. Have you heard of Pilat-"

"Specialist, punch him again. We don't have time for this."

The soldier slugged John in his stomach again. John threw up and started crying.

"Let me talk to him," said Jason to Gemma. "Hey, we're with the good guys here. He's not going to punch you again but we're on an urgent mission here and we can't fuck around. Do you know who I am?"

"Yeah," blubbered John between his gasping sobs.

"Okay. That's a start. What's your name?"

"John…" he blubbered again.

"What are you doing here, John? Are you a missionary or something?"

"No. I'm looking for someone."

"Who are you looking for, John?" Jason asked as he crouched down to gain eye contact with the detainee.

"You seriously shouldn't fuck with me. Whoever punched me is going to have his nuts ripped off by me."

The specialist raised his fist to punch John again.

"Specialist Luther, that's enough," barked Gemma.

"Good. Specialist Luther. Now I know his name," said John as he wiped his tears away.

"John, come on. We need your help here. What's it going to take?"

"I'm going to fucking shoot him, Jason," Growled Specialist Luther.

"Don't. I told you, I got this. John, tell me. What do you want? I can hook it up. I'm filthy rich. All we need to know is why you're here and Mutobo isn't. Simple as that."

"Help me up."

Jason's Powersuit whirred as he helped John back to his feet. John's arm shot out at the crotch of the soldier who had punched him twice. His fingers clenched viciously around the testicles of the man and the man screamed a blood curling scream those rose above the treetops and out into the Universe. Gemma pistol-whipped John before Jason could intercede, causing him to lose consciousness. Legions of fans screamed in delight in Jason's ear and "John" and "nuts" became the most searched terms in the digital world for the next hour. "Jesus, Gemma. There's a time and a place. For all we know, this guy was probably a missionary or a monk of some kind. We're not any closer to finding out where the fuck Mutobo is!"

"Forrest. Daniels. Take Specialist Luther to Medevac and lift him out of here. I don't want a man bleeding out on my watch."

Gemma cleaned a small bit of blood off of her pistol.

"We'll take him back to base and have someone question him there. He's obviously not important in any of this. Some bumbling tablet salesman or something. Somepiece of shit with a fast right hand that showed up at the wrong time," she said.

"Yeah, his face isn't turning up in my registry. At least tell me ahead of time if you're going to do something like that so I can frame it up."

Jason slung John's limp body into the lead helicopter and both he and Gemma climbed in. They would have plenty of time to learn more about this bizarre "John" character when he came to his senses.

"They found Mutobo!" yelled the pilot.

"What?" Gemma yelled back over the noise of the spinning rotor and its blades.

Jason had his hand to his ear. He leaned over and spoke in her ear, "Mutobo. He's leading an attack on the dam. He and his sub commander are trying to break into the dam."

The helicopter shot up into the sky and hurried to the dam. It took Gemma and the rest of the convoy nearly four minutes before they noticed one of the helicopters in the rear did not leave the camp.

Chapter 28

Arnold's shoulders were slowly getting tired from carrying Charlie and Joanna. A voice in his head remarkably similar to John's, starting grunting to him, "200 more yards. Give me 200 more yards." He thought of when he had to carry John the last six miles of a fifty mile hike because John's ankles were too bloodied for him to continue. His own strength had faltered momentarily when their drill sergeant forced John to carry his own pack while Arnold carried him. Both dug deep and finished the hike. They spent three days in the infirmary.

In the infirmary there was a nurse named Luz who would come into their room from time to time to clean their bandages or pass out anti-inflammatories. Arnold had been raised by racist parents and therefore had little interest in this Mexican-Texan woman. John had not been raised racist, nor could he afford to discriminate. Any human with a vagina over the age of sixteen was fair game. He had once, as a high school student, read in a book titled *Samantha's Secrets* that women are more prone to be aroused in the early evening. There were illustrated images of a woman wearing a pinstripe suit and smoking through a cigarette holder. It was a comic book.

On the second early evening of their stay in the infirmary, John sprung his trap on Luz.

"Hi Luz," he winked at her as she walked into their room with a tray.

"Buenas noches, Señor Macy," she chirped at him as she set down a cup of water for Arnold.

He was irked by her misstep but continued.

"You know, Ms. Garcia, I was just thinking a little bit about when I visited Texas just after high school. I was telling Arnold about how I learned how to focus my personality energy onto different points in my body. Wasn't I, Arnold?"

Arnold nodded vigorously as they had rehearsed many times before. Luz did not seem impressed.

"You were in Te-has?" she asked cautiously.

"What?"

"You said you were in Te-has. Here you go."

"I was there, yeah. Doing some really important work on myself."

"What city you were working in?"

"Huh? No. As I was saying, I figured a way to control blood flow to different points in my body thanks to the personality channeling I learned from a nice old Mexican lady. Probably could have been your mom!"

Luz gave John a blank look of confusion before turning to leave.

"Can I ask you something, Ms. Garcia?"

"Dee-meh"

"You don't have to be so short with me," he pouted.

"Que? I don't have time for dis. Leave me alone now. I have to go. And please don't touch your hand against me when I give your water, is hairy and I'm not attracted to you."

Arnold smiled to himself with a hint of pride as he considered how much John had improved in talking to women since their boot camp days. Charlie and Joanna felt lighter on his muscles for a moment. The last time he had been able to convince John to go to the Aubame's, John managed to dance with a girl for almost three minutes before she left the brothel to get back to her pineapple stand across the street.

When John was a boy, he learned how to dance by watching a cartoon. At least this was what he told Arnold. Sometimes they watched cartoons together at the plantation when it was too hot to work outside. This cartoon became one of their favorites. In the cartoon, the bullfighter assumed the stance of a flamenco dancer as a Spanish guitar song played. The bullfighter circled the bull in this stiff stance, one hand in the air above his head and the other near his waist as if he had an imaginary towel draped over his forearm. The bull stood on his hooves and danced with the bullfighter. John called this the "Bullfighter Move" to Arnold when he decided they should practice dancing at the plantation after a caffeine-fueled cartoon marathon. Arnold learned the move with a lot of enthusiasm and was eager to see John perform the move on a girl sometime later.

"There's a supernova of lightning here and there's one over there and boop!" giggled Charlie. He was drooling down Arnold's back.

"Tell me about it. Who do you think this buffalo is? John hired him," mumbled Joanna.

Arnold was getting annoyed with their babbling. It all felt very false. He could see that they had hardly ever embarked on any psychedelic trips before, maybe a shared joint in a circle of people at a house party. Thumbprinting them was a massive mistake but he was determined to keep them cozy for the next 48 hours. Sleep wasn't going to wipe away their trips.

A group of six helicopters zoomed by overhead. Arnold dropped down and gently rolled John's friends off his shoulders. They gurgled and became silent as the sensation of cold jungle soil enveloped every thread of their nervous systems. Ants crawled onto Charlie's leg. He embodied a childhood memory and closed his eyes.

Arnold left his daytrippers to rest and set out for a wooden shack he spied far off in the distance. His shoulders readjusted to their normal size as he sprinted along what he knew to be John's foot tracks. The soles of those sandals were unmistakable. All of the other tracks in the area were over a day old. The sudden realization that the helicopters had not only landed, but were preparing to take off again set off his alarm bells. He considered his best friend's utter uselessness in combat. He remembered the rifles he had left in the trunk of a tree and furrowed his brow.

The shack provided him enough cover to venture a peek into the rebel camp. He saw the helicopters taking off, with John being thrown into a Black Hawk by a man in a strange suit. Something roared inside of Arnold and he took off after the nearest helicopter. It was the last to take off and he caught it just as it was leaving the ground. A gunner yelled in surprise as Arnold flung his body into the man at full speed. The soldiers sitting on the chairs within the helicopter grabbed ahold of the massive man. He tore their throats out with a flick of the knife had taken out someone's ankle holster. The pilot screamed in agony as he hit the ground and suffered compound fractures to both his femurs. Arnold was now piloting the helicopter.

Chapter 29

"Home sweet home," Higgins thought to himself as he approached the Jeep. His precious family was waiting inside, hopefully with food and drink. He had worn himself thin on this brief adventure. A friendly tropical bird who owed him a favor brought him a large part of the way home. The mud from a small flood around the plantation had slowed his progress upon being set down. The limp is in his leg was worse than it had ever been. His tail dragged in the dirt. It had been a great puzzle to him to return to the plantation and not see a single sign of the two humans anywhere. Usually the large oaf would be asleep near the goats or somewhere nearby, trying to lift himself into a tree over and over. The smaller man was always in a hut, muttering to himself. Higgins couldn't see either of them.

As soon as he crawled his way up into the interior of the Jeep and set his paws on the solid metal floor of his home, he was engulfed by his adoring children. They smothered him with affectionate nuzzles and licked at the ginger spots on his tail. His wife beamed at him from across the engine compartment. He was finally home! There was a great feast of miracle berries, grains and vegetables stolen from the kitchen on the plantation, and Higgins' favorite: goat's milk. As sleep settled in on the family, a brief snooze before the night's great activities, Higgins began to think to himself, "I am getting to be an old timer now. It's time to hang up the gloves and step out of the ring. My day has passed and now I got to look to the future. My children are my future. That damn cat was a dangerous bastard but he's never going to hurt my babies, that much is certain. These children need me. My wife needs me for making more pups so I'm going to stay put in this house and make it happen. I'm lucky I found her, a good woman who is okay with being with a smart man like me. The world needs more mega-mice, mice that will grow up with their daddies around. That's something I never had."

His goals had never been as clear to him as that moment. He fell into a deep sleep and dreamt about his mother's unconditional love.

Higgins lived to be very old and satisfied in the life he lived on the plantation. There was never again a threat to his family for as long as they lived in the Jeep. He and his wife went on to produce seven more litters of mice. She was a sturdy and noble presence for the family but knew her intellectual limitations. Higgins took to the habit of stealing away moments in the hut to study the human possessions. This broadened his knowledge. He imparted this knowledge to his children and they went on to propagate across the valley the largest community of mega-mice in the world. When Higgins died, he was remembered as the mouse that escaped the genocide across the Ocean, outsmarted and tamed the predators, and spread philosophy through enlightened parenting to dozens of hybrid mice. His funeral was attended by hundreds of mice and guarded by a legion of gray parrots. His last act had been to unite the smartest bird and the smartest mammal on the continent at a monthly lyceum on the plantation grounds.

Chapter 30

A cool breeze lapped across John's face. He was in a great hall. The floors were made of large marble slabs. Great columns rose up into a darkened ceiling beyond his vision. Statues of great figures in the history of philosophy and self-help lined a magnificent burgundy carpet. Within the carpet were golden fibers and filaments that dazzled before his eyes.

He focused his eyes and could see images of giggling babies within their reflections. He gazed up the length of the carpet and marveled at the massive round stone table that lay some distance ahead upon a raised platform. As he made his way to the table, cats and coyotes with feathered wings flitted in and out of his field of vision. They were playing orchestral instruments with their bejeweled paws. John felt very happy and warm in his chest. He waved to a cat that looked a lot like Rupert. The Rupert cat winked back at John as he floated up, up, and away.

Soon John was at the table. He walked to the grandest of the thrones circling the table and sat himself down. It was a throne made of elephant ivory with purple velvet plush for cushions. He rubbed his hands around the arms of the throne and felt a swelling of pride. This throne felt just right. A series of people flickered into the other five thrones at the table. John could see his mother in her yoga clothes, a wolf in humanoid form wearing silver armor, a large black man with dreadlocks wearing a black suit and holding a saxophone, a slender teenager with a patchy beard and a skateboard, and a man seated opposite of him who looked very similar to him. He focused on the man and saw he was wearing a blue plaid shirt, a tan colored down vest, and mullet with sandy blonde hair. The man gave him a menacing look. John returned the look with equal defiance.

"The Great Council has been called to session," announced the large black man.

"Let us pause for our fallen comrades," grunted the wolf.

The characters at the round table bowed their heads in genuflection, all except John and one other.

"Are we praying? Cause if so, count me out," said the patchy-bearded skateboarder.

"Okay. Joke's up, people. Where are we and who the heck are you? Hi, Mom."

John gave a curt nod to his mother.

"John, we are The Great Council. We are your mightiest warriors. You have assembled us in this place because there is a great danger coming. Our path is the warpath and all legions have been recalled from their peaceful places to bear arms," said the wolf.

"Right…where is Arnold? This place is *waaaaay* too nice to be in Zabon. Did Arnold drug me again?"

"Son, we are in you," said his mother.

"What the fuck? Seriously? Arnold! Arnold! Rupert, kitty-kitty. Come here, kitty-kitty."

The black man rang out a piercing note on his saxophone.

"Oh…" John muttered. "I get it now."

"Thank you," the five others chimed in unison.

"I get why you all are here but who the fuck is he?" He pointed at the man seated across from him.

"Who the fuck are you, hombre?" the man across from him spit right back.

"Please allow us to introduce ourselves," said the man in the suit. "I am the Big Boss. I am the owner and operator of the Crystal Palace. You mostly see me when you are singing to music or teaching Arnold and yourself how to dance. I love a good meal and some good tunes, haha!" The Big Boss folded his hands across his belly and chuckled deeply.

"I am The Protector Woman," said the woman that looked like his mother. "I wield two ravens."

Two ravens flickered into existence on either of her shoulders. One was bright red and the other was a deep grey with a yellow beak.

"This raven is Shame." She raised her hand to her left shoulder and then let it drop down again. The grey raven bowed to John. "This raven is Scorn." The red raven screeched at John.

"What the fuck-" he gasped.

"I am currently the operator of The Kitchen but someday I would like to run an orphanage or perhaps become a children's author. You mostly see me when you are dealing with feelings of rejection and unworthiness. We have plenty more work to do together in the coming years."

"I'm Rebel" said the patchy-bearded skateboarder.

"Of course! That makes so much sense," said John, rolling his eyes.

"We play video games together-"

"No we don't."

"Yeah we do. You probably just don't know it yet."

"Uh, sure."

"Do you want me to tell you more about me or not?" said Rebel.

"Go on."

"Like I said, we play video games together. As my name implies, I'm around when there someone messing with us. We don't take shit from anybody and nobody is going to tell us what to do. Silver Wolf and I work pretty closely together on that one. We're actually the main generals of the armies. I handle logistics, thanks to my video game skills, and he handles brute power and might. Can I get a small request in? We need to build a skate park at the Plantation or something. My legs are getting noodly from all the Pilates."

"You don't like Pilates?" the Protector Woman said to Rebel.

"No. Not really. It's okay but it doesn't give me much excitement."

"I didn't know that. Thanks for telling me," she replied.

"The pleasure is all mine," said Rebel. "I'd like to let Silver Wolf speak now if that's okay with you, John."

"Why would it be up to me?" he asked. "I guess he could talk if he wanted."

"Thank you, John," said Silver Wolf. "I eat rabbits. Snatch their pelts with my jaws and rip em'. I am the Fireblood and the steel trap. I am the force in the wind. I am the howling at the moon. Rebel directs and I flow. It is an honor to speak to you again, Commander Rock."

John was tickled by being addressed as a commander. He was still very confused but things were becoming clearer to him.

"Let me see if I can get this straight. You're all people inside of me and there's trouble coming. We're meeting because we need to plan ahead somehow."

"We could all die," said The Big Boss.

"Grave danger," said Silver Wolf.

"Who's going to take charge?" asked John.

"I am," said the man across from John. He put on a pair of aviator glasses and stood up. "We need to fuck these pussies in the butt. It's the Rockin' Lifestyle, right?"

The four other heads of the armies clapped vigorously.

"We don't really have a plan but we don't need a plan because we're the tits. That's the plan," the man smirked as he spoke.

There was applause all around the table again. A few coyotes and cats fluttered into view and approved of the announcement as well.

"Wait…what? Who are you, buddy?" asked John.

"I should ask you the same question. You wanna' go?" threatened the man.

John felt a wave of uncertainty wash over him. He looked to the Protector Woman for help but she was gazing at the mystery man with a look of intense approval. The Big Boss was snacking on a ham sandwich and bumping elbows with Rebel. They were looking at the man.

"Yeah, I'll go," John said as he stood up. The stone table mechanically lowered into the floor was obscured by two burgundy carpeted panels that came together.

"Oh shit, man, my tilapia stew!" groaned The Big Boss as he tried to reach down at a bowl on the table as it lowered down. John snapped his fingers and a bowl of stew appeared in the big man's hands. "Thanks, brother!"

"I got you, BB," said John. He noticed that the Big Boss had shifted some of his focus away from the mystery man.

"Gentlemen," said Rebel as he presented the mystery man and John with a Nintendo LTS each. "-please switch on your LTS and stand at your podium.

Two podiums rose up from the edge of the platform. The thrones floated away and the generals took their places behind the two competitors. In the direction they were facing, a massive hologram appeared thirty feet beyond the podiums. A game of Fizzle snapped into view. Candles on great chandeliers were lit by flying coyotes and cats. The winged creatures settled into two grandstands on either sides of the enormous hologram.

John squinted to see the foam fingers and banners the creatures were holding. The foam fingers on his side were white with black fringes and featured the pointer finger extending from the hand. The banners were littered with phrases such as "Rockin' Hard!" and "Arnold and Rupert Second Team". John looked across to the other grandstand. The foam fingers were black with white fringes and featured the middle finger extending from the hand. The phrases were "I don't think so!" and "Not in my house!" This bewildered John.

He looked behind himself and could see that Rebel, Silver Wolf, and The Protector Woman with both her ravens were standing behind the mystery man. The Big Boss winked at him and then put a hand on John's shoulder. His touch felt like a deep, sonorous rumbling. John smiled the purest smile he had felt in years and looked forward at the hologram. This was the final battle of Fizzle.

A cool breeze came across John again and he felt his eyelids open. He saw red in one of his eyes and touched it gingerly. He was in the air. There were boots next to him. He was on a floor. There was a set of red boots with glimmering green electronic veins. He let his one good eye travel up the length of the boot and towards a sympathetic face that was smiling down on him.

"You're Jason Christmas!"

"Looks like he's up" said Jason to Gemma.

"Where are we going? Am I on Christmas Vision?"

"Sure are, buddy."

"What's your last name," barked Gemma.

"Where's the Fizzle match I was playing? Where's my LTS?"

Fizzle roared from #129,399 on the Rio bestseller list to #5 in Jason's heads up display. Museums across Asia began auctioning LTS units.

"What do you know about Mutobo?"

"I don't know where Mutobo is. Why is my head bloody?"

"What were you trying to sell him? What church are you working for?"

"Church? Rock don't play like that. False spiritualism dies in the face of self-knowledge. Come on, is this the 20th Century or something?"

"Who is Rock?" asked Jason.

"That's my last name, thanks for asking politely." John leered at Gemma.

Jason leaned against Gemma to pull her attention away from John. She felt arousal as the warmth of the Powersuit tickled her skin.

"That's John Rock."

"He said that much. Who is he and what the fuck was he doing at the insurgent base of operations?"

"CM is telling me he's the US Army's most hated man. Something about kidnapping a Colonel. John Rock is his alias. Private John Macy until he went AWOL at an awards banquet. Went completely off the radar with one Private First Class Colfax. Left a trail of dead black ops hunters until the Army pulled out from West Africa. Gemma, this is a really fucking dangerous guy. Luther's nuts are in a bag full of ice right now cause of this guy. He didn't learn that groin rip in the Army. He could be an insurgent. We need to secure him in a holding cell on base or at least put him in a restraint bubble until we can get back."

"I have never heard of this-"

"Excuse me, Mr. Bigshot!" yelled John. "You didn't acknowledge my point. False spiritualism is a byproduct of ignorance of the psychological processes that determine our emotional makeup at any given moment. Essentially, it is a tool for manipulation that a person with an unadjusted narcissistic disorder will employ to either ensure a continuous feedback loop of narcissistic supply or substantive monetary support from large groups of viewers and well-wishers. You probably know this all too well, being the public persona that you are. What you don't know is that the longer you live in this manner, the harder it becomes for you to connect with the truth of your emotions. Luke Fitzgibbons tell us in his masterpiece work *Honest Communication* that if we allow ourselves to see the cult of personality in the greater world in front of our eyes, we can begin to examine the cult of personality within ourselves that we 'cult'-ivate at the expense of our inner child."

"That's really interesting, Private Macy," hissed Gemma. John seemed to shudder and his eyes rolled into the back of his head.

"I see the 'Gun in the Room' and you happen to be holding it so I'm going to let that one slide but I'm warning you, Missy: my *name is John Rock.*"

"You know what socialism would say about your theory?" she replied.

Jason was surprised and impressed by the sudden appearance of intellect. He had thought she was little more than a killing machine with perfect breasts.

"I can wager a fair guess but I'm not going to," said John.

"Pure socialism would say that the theories of Luke Fitzgibbons don't take into account that man is born fundamentally flawed-"

"Bullshit! I call bullshit!" John looked to the other soldiers in the helicopter for approval.

The other soldiers were confused by their superiors' willingness to engage the prisoner right before a heavy fire fight. They shrugged their shoulders and listened in.

John took a deep breath and began to gesture with his hands as he spoke. He was sitting up at this point. "I am feeling annoyed and the thought is I know all too well where you're going to go with this. I do also feel some curiosity and the thought is that maybe we can work something out. Please, continue."

"As Thomas Hobbes proved in his seminal work *Leviathan*, there is a need for a strong central government or men would be at constant war with his fellow man. We have seen time and time again-"

"Commander Wayne, our ETA is fifteen minutes. Commander Sutherland has sent reinforcements from all outposts in Yellow Zone" radioed the pilot.

"Thank you, Bishop. Time and time again there have been despots that have stoked local fanaticism into regional unrest and eventually open warfare. Men like your friend Mutobo have led to the slaughter of millions of innocent civilians time and time again. Mutobo is an African

Mussolini. He is a murderer and we're going to put him down like the dog he is. We are the Churchill to his Adolf Hitler. We are the Sam Donaldson to his Ignacio Ponce. We are the peacemakers of the world and the world pays the United Nations a lot of money to make sure that peace is held. Man's nature is evil. History has proven that we cannot leave man to his own devices. Fitzgibbons' nonsense about self-knowledge and a stateless world is impossible to translate into the real world. He's a utopian. He runs a cult. Self-knowledge is for the losers that no one liked in high school. Join the real world, Private Rock. Your cult is deluded and led by a man who shames others for not buying enough of his t-shirts. I mean, my God, could you weak minded men be anymore homosexually drawn into your false father figure?"

Jason nodded furiously as Gemma said the word 'cult'. He brought up his ScatterRifle to his field of vision and captured a commercial with Fizzle sensation John Rock in the background.

"Wow! You're crazy, lady. You went from 'pure socialism' to 'Thomas Hobbes' to 'Mutobo and Mussolini' to calling Lu a cult leader. At no point in your incoherent ramblings reminiscent of the kind of goat manure we keep at the plantation did you string together even the semblance of an argument. Fie on your unsound mind and your distasteful use of Statist jargon. Karl Marx is in his deep grave right now, literally choking up on his cereal chunks because of your-"

Gemma drew her pistol and shot at John. Jason reacted at exactly the right moment and saved John's life by deflecting her arm. He knocked the pistol from her hand. John urinated himself. The soldiers laughed at him. He rolled his eyes back into his head again and composed himself.

"I feel so humiliated right now. This really hurts."

Gemma and Jason murmured to each other for a couple minutes before turning their attention back to John. Jason spoke first.

"Commander Wayne has agreed not to kill you but only because we guaranteed her a portion of the proceeds you're going to make from being the Master of Ceremonies of the first Fizzle tournament in sixteen years! How do you feel, John?"

"I feel pretty confused and a little hungry. Where are you taking me?"

"Come on, you're on contract with Christmas Media now John. I'm going to take care of you."

"Did you say Commander '*Wayne*'? Like a man's name?"

A Shenzhen Arms salesperson buzzed in Jason's ear, asking him to see if John was available in the next few weeks provided he wasn't in a General Utility Correctional Facility.

"Commander Gemma Wayne herself. She took over for Sutherland just a little bit ago. Best damn UN commander if you ask me." Jason laughed artificially and sent his endorsement to Coca Cola.

John studied Gemma's pixie haircut. She was busy relaying orders over her communicator implants, readying the few reinforcements at the dam for the arrival of the helicopters. He noticed her freckles and began to have an erection. The fact that she had just tried to kill him was completely gone from his memory. She turned to look over her shoulder and bark an order at the side gunner. Rebels were entering their sector of fire. John saw the scar Joanna had described to him. This was his chance to get a girlfriend! He remembered from *Seduction Guide* that woman liked honesty.

"Gemma Wayne?" he called to her over the roar of the heavy machine gun that piecing apart a rebel pickup.

"What do you want, Piss Pants?"

"I've been looking for you."

"I'm busy. You're going to be cuffed to the floor until we retake the dam. Try not to pee yourself again."

"Charlie and Joanne hired me to find you. That's why I was at Mutobo's."

Gemma motioned to two soldiers to cuff him. She leaned in to say something to John as the helicopter took up a landing pattern.

"You're going to have to tell me about that la-"

"I want to have sex with you," John said in his most seductive voice.

Jason powered up his Suit and pretended not to hear what John said. Gemma uncomfortably turned her attention to the firefight below. She readied her weaponry and began giving directions to everyone on board but John.

John closed his eyes and pretended to meditate. He was feeling bitterly rejected.

Chapter 31

There was not a single shred of knowledge in Arnold's brain of how to pilot a helicopter. This fact did not dawn on him until the moment his hand gripped the joystick. The vehicle did not respond the way he expected it to when he tried to steer it. He rose higher and higher until the prospect of jumping out and onto a tree turned deadly.

The helicopter leveled out and hovered in place. He left the seat and looked among the dead bodies of the soldiers for some rope or a parachute of some kind. There was nothing. For the first time since he was a little boy in a corral with an angry bull, Arnold panicked. The panic was short lived, however. He spotted a strange looking jumpsuit made of stretchable material. It looked to have a parachute pack built into the material. He read the lone insignia on the suit: Powersuit III. John had briefly talked about the Powersuit at one point. Really, he had railed against it as being "contrary to the evolutionary path of the human body" or something like that. The Powersuit wasn't going to help him get down from the helicopter but it would help him run really fast. He slipped it on. It conformed to his body and seemed to power up.

A yellow tint came over his vision and the word "Offline" flashed in front of him twice. Arnold thought of how to turn the suit's power on and scratched his hip. The moment he did so his legs felt a surge of strength. He scratched both of his arms and they felt like they were made of titanium. He popped his neck and felt a powerful hardening develop around his head. He looked over the edge of the helicopter and down into the jungle canopy below. A red tint in his eyesight flashed to life and he saw a digital schematic mapping the perfect location for him to jump for. He obliged the advanced knowledge that had dawned on him so conveniently moments before.

Arnold was able to remain within earshot of the helicopters. His HUD told him he was leaping at 95 miles per hour and would completely drain the battery in 2 hours. It didn't matter to him. He needed to save his best friend. If the suit ran out of energy, he would steal a boat and keep going up the Bura after the kidnappers.

He kept slamming into trees and slipping over trunks. The going was much easier and less painful once he reached the shores of the river. The helicopters were heading straight for the dam. He tapped his head the same way he always did in football to pump himself up. The hardened suit made him feel like he had a helmet and pads on again. A blinking diagram of a brain came up on his HUD and showed him several block spots labeled with complicated language he didn't understand. A jolt of the most comforting sensation he'd ever had come over his nervous system. He began to understand the labels. The suit was showing him the brain damage he'd suffered from the concussions he went through in football and the spankings he endured as a boy on his parents' farm. Black spots turned purple, then blue, then green and he understood the light spectrum for the first time in two decades. A giddy pleasure was restored to him. His legs surged forward after the helicopters with a passionate zeal.

Chapter 32

Walter fired through a glass window and into the body of a UN soldier trying to close a set of security doors. The doors remained open. Several rebels prowled into the room with their rifles raised. The few remaining UN soldiers on the far side of the chamber raised their arms in surrender. Their weapons were confiscated and they were made to sit on the floor with wrists cuffed behind their backs. Mutobo smiled at Walter and patted his back. Walter flinched, remembering their encounter from earlier in the day. Mutobo didn't notice. Adrenaline and the lingering effects from his drunken morning were clouding his head.

"Dam is clear. Bring it in," Mutobo spoke into a communicator.

Louis, a short and stout explosives specialist, strode into the chamber a half minute later. He was wearing a large black backpack. Walter signaled for three men to sweep the turbine room while the timed bomb was readied. Louis unslung the backpack. He set it on the floor and began to pull a large rectangular case from its main compartment.

"Are you okay, Lion?" he asked Mutobo as he glanced up at his superior.

"I am feeling tired, Louis. My wife and daughter are dead. This is the last of it for me."

"Yes, Lion. Are you thirsty, Sir?"

"Thank you."

The urgency of the moment retook them as their radios notified them that enemy helicopters were less than three minutes away. Walter took two subordinates and the shackled prisoners out of the chamber. Louis connected a pair of cables into the bomb and switched it on. The three soldiers returned from their sweep of the turbine room.

"How long, Sir?"

"Give it ten minutes. I'll set it myself. Now get out of here and go help with the RPGs!"

Walter returned to the chamber.

"Why did you send Louis out? He can do it, Lion. You are too valuable to be here doing it yourself. Wayne is on her way and we need your rifle."

"You know why I am staying, Walta'"

"Damn it, Mutobo! You are not a hero, not today. I'm getting Louis."

Walter turned and ran to retrieve the explosives specialist. Mutobo quickly walked to the turbine room, carrying the bomb, and locked himself in by destroying the keypad on his side after the door slid shut. Walter returned with Louis and pounded on the window helplessly as they watched Mutobo walk away. They pulled themselves away from the window. Reports of chain gun fire were coming in from troops stationed around the helicopter hangar.

Mutobo was blubbering to himself.

The UN soldiers trapped in the helicopter hangar were using a mounted chain gun to tear a hole in the side of the hangar large enough to be uncoverable by rebel fire. It was a stupid, pointless plan but they persisted and were lucky enough to see their stunt draw away rebels from the dam entrance. This coincided with the arrival of Gemma Wayne, Jason Christmas, and their attack helicopters. All hell broke loose. Reinforcements for the United Nations forces and the Zabonese rebels were pouring into the valley. Young men with hunting rifles who wanted to take pot-shots at blue helmeted outsiders came. Children who wanted to run ammunition belts and grenades to entrenched rebels scampered through the jungle. 50 caliber machine guns mounted on the backs of pickups rumbled through the valley, stopping to skirmish with incoming UN convoys. Thousands of combatants were firing on each other. It was the largest ground battle on the continent in forty years. Both sides were annihilating each other.

With 60 feet left to descend, a generational icon wearing his Powersuit IV leapt to the ground and landed with calculated precision. His ScatterRifle spun around from his back and into his outstretched hands. The Rifle fired whistling globs of green projectiles indiscriminately. Gemma

Wayne watched from above in curious horror at the carnage he was inflicting. She noticed he was shooting at UN soldiers.

"What the fuck are you doing?" she bellowed through her communicator to him

"Yeah, right, Shenzhen Arms and GU have me on retainer. The UN Council refused to sign the combat agreement so it's fair game!"

"You're not going to shoot the helicopters down are you?"

"No, Gemma. You and I have a dinner to get to in a week. Can't risk blowing up your pretty face!" he shouted over the hammering of bullets against his suit's armor.

Gemma blushed. She remembered what John had just said to her and glanced at him. He had one eye slightly open and trained on her. He noticed her glance in his direction and tried to give her a 'thumbs up' signal. His arms caught when his handcuff chains ran out of slack.

"I would love to go out to dinner with you, Jason," she said loudly.

John started breathing heavily. Jealousy made its way through his system. He decided he was going to try and get her alone and reason with her, to show her his virtue. She needed a moral man in her life.

The ScatterRifle was performing beautifully for Jason. He smiled as he allowed a billionaire bidder to assume remote control of the Powersuit IV for thirty seconds. He allowed his body to go completely limp and marveled as the billionaire fumbled away his precious time by electing to fire at a series of treetops. To his credit, a large part of a tree did land in front of a pair of rebels. The rebels used the tree as cover to fire upon an armored vehicle that had just joined the fray.

His Suit gave him control and he began narrating the footage he was recording.

"Well, folks, you are seeing firsthand the wallop the ScatterRifle packs. Christmas Media is going to be offering, in a joint venture with Shenzhen Arms, a combo pack for a limited time. We're going to get you going with a working, combat version of the Powersuit III and the beta version of the ScatterRifle. The combat Powersuit has previously been unavailable to the general public, as you all know. In celebration of this special release, we are going to be offering free Pleasure Time through Climax Bubble for the first ten thousand pre-orders. Every pre-order up to the first one hundred thousand is going to be entered into a special drawing where the grand prize winner will win a free round trip flight to a place of my choice. There the winner will be put up in luxury accommodation thanks to Ivory Yurts. Ivory Yurts: the choice for foldable luxury on-the-go. In your accommodation you will be given ten hours of fitness training from one of my top-tier trainers. From there you will either get to meet me, Jason Christmas, for a pre-arranged mercenary firefight in a Powersuit or you will get to have sex with Leslie Kimble, twelve time Olympic gold medalist in track and field. Of course, if we have a female grand prize winner, I am willing to lend my body out to the good cause!"

Delighted laughter burst into his ears from headquarters. A live graph, tracking his pre-order sales, came up on his HUD. Leslie Kimble congratulated the billionaire on his "skilled marksmanship" from her villa in the Swiss Alps.

"Uh oh, looks like John is getting away," spoke a control tech monitoring the Suit's rear optics from headquarters.

Jason turned around to see John picking the lock to his second handcuff.

"Attach a flysight to him and we'll see where he goes. This guy is seriously a star," said the tech.

Jason stopped his onslaught for a moment to aim his forearm at John. A small camera launched from the PowerSuit IV and flew several hundred yards to John's burgundy shirt. It attached itself to his collar and conformed to the burgundy color. A video feed appeared in the bottom left corner of Jason's HUD, aptly titled the "Rock Cam." Five second Fizzle commercials graced the feed at 45 second intervals. The United States Army was prepared to offer clemency to Private John Macy in exchange for free advertising on the "Rock Cam."

Arnold arrived to the battlefield. He knew enough about the armed conflict between the Zabonese Regular Army and its ally, the United Nations, and the rebel groups in the country to rudimentarily grasp the carnage before him. He decided to disarm anyone between him and John in order to reduce the chances any damage could come to his best friend. His Powersuit scanned the dam and registered another Powersuit user, a Version 4 user. The last person he had seen John with was wearing a Powersuit. He plotted a course to intercept the kidnapper.

 Bullets were soon bouncing against several points on his body, causing him discomfort. Three UN soldiers had their rifles snatched away from them and tied into a knot. They ran screaming in terror but were tackled and relieved of their sidearms and all other potential dangerous objects. Arnold proceeded to knock them out with a brief punch to each chin. He could see on his thermal display that there were 50 heat registers between him and John's kidnapper. He spent the next half hour laughing to himself, springing out of the treetops onto unsuspecting combatants, and marveling at the strength the Powersuit gave him every time he ruined a weapon. This was the happiest he had felt in a long time. It felt like such a mistake to kill people in the past when he could have much more fun tackling them and breaking their little guns. After a while, Arnold forgot all about rescuing John and became engrossed in disarming anyone he saw. For some reason it felt *right* to him to do it.

Walter was trapped near the dam entrance. Gemma had him pinned down with two fire squads of Blue Berets. They both knew that one of them was going to die. Pleas to lay down arms came from his communicator. Two men in Powersuits were tearing through the battlefield. One was killing everyone. The other was stealing guns. It made no sense. The rebels were scared for the first time in their lives.

"I'm going. Come on, Walter," Louis screamed over the noise of covering fire.

Walter reached out to pull him back under cover but it was too late. Louis sprinted across the open ground to a security post but was gunned down before he made it. Walter retreated to safety behind a wall and cursed out loud. There was no way he was getting out but there was no way the UN soldiers were getting in. He was the stopgap between the freedom of Bura Valley and its enslavement by General Utility and the United Nations. He reloaded his weapons in time to cut down a Blue Beret trying to sneak up on him. This elicited renewed heavy fire from Gemma Wayne's soldiers.

Gemma congratulated herself after she shot an insurgent running for cover. Over her communicator, Jason was narrating his movements. He was beginning to notice that some of the soldiers and insurgents he was shooting were unarmed and disabled. She noticed that only one insurgent lay between her and the dam entrance. The man was well-entrenched behind a thick wall. She sent a Blue Beret with stealth enhancements to flush him out. It didn't work. She was about to order her fire squads to toss all available grenades when she noticed a brave soul slither his way out of the bush and over a retaining wall. It was John Rock. He was sneaking into the dam almost completely undetected.

"How the fuck does he do it?" wondered Gemma aloud.

The insurgent behind the wall took no notice of John but instead tossed a perfectly aimed grenade that blew apart two more of Gemma's men. She took her attention away from John, who didn't seem to notice the intense firefight he was leaving behind, and ordered Jason to come assist her.

Chapter 33

A giddy fear overtook John as he jumped down from his careful jungle hike and into plain view in front of the dam entrance. This was the bravest thing he had ever done and he had self-knowledge to thank for it. His emotions were clearly on his side. He was using his elevated consciousness to navigate the dangers of the battlefield and make his way to where he presumed Gemma would be. On his way to the dam he had come across a child soldier. The child giggled in delight to see John, recognizing him from the schoolhouse visit the day before. They hugged and the boy silently pointed John in the direction of the dam. Unbeknownst to John, the boy saved his life by alerting all of the other rebels in the immediate vicinity that the Nintendo employee with the funny shirt was trying to get to Mutobo to help him set up the bomb. It was a brazen lie but child soldiers were less immune to fairytales, despite all their traumas.

The plan of seduction with Gemma was going to be simple. John had already stated his desire of having sex with her. In his increased empathetic state, he detected a hint of gamesmanship from her when she made sure he heard her accept Jason's offer of a romantic dinner. This told John that Gemma was at least willing to try and get some jealousy out of him. According to Dr. Walter Reilly, author of *Games Women Play*, this meant there were two reasonable responses to her game. John could either react by using his emotional state as a conclusion to try and manage her emotions or he could see the inner child in her and be sure to gain that child's trust before pursuing his desire. The solution was simple: getting Gemma to relax by playing Fizzle would allow her sexuality to express itself without fear of judgment. This meant finding Gemma (who was probably in the dam somewhere), tricking her into being alone by agreeing to an interrogation, and then introducing the toy for her inner child to play with (the Nintendo LTS).

His anticipation was replaced confusion as he saw there wasn't a single living soul in the dam complex. There were many spent shell casings laying on the ground and evidence of many gun battles, yet no Gemma

Wayne. John felt very confused. He needed to sit down. He also needed to pee so he found a bathroom. As he sat down on a toilet he felt a momentary flash of insecurity for sitting when he only needed to "go number one." He thought about where Gemma could possibly be. He realized that he was going to need to customize a new character for her in Fizzle and lower the difficulty levels.

Five minutes went by and John was thoroughly engrossed in a new game of Fizzle with the character he created for his love interest. He snapped out of it and renewed his search for Gemma. This led him to the exterior of the turbine room. The sliding door to the room was broken. He found a crawlspace and made his way through it. Giddy feelings took him over again as he imagined seeing Gemma naked on a couch as he exited the crawlspace on the other side. No such fantasy awaited him as he emerged from a grated door into the turbine room. There was nothing but the hum of machinery and the gentle rush of water.

"Chinese design, no bypass circuits, and a delay trigger for remote demo jobs. Nice!" he exclaimed as he approached a man sitting next to a large bomb. He put the LTS in his pocket.

The man whirled around with a pistol in his hand. John put his hands up.

"Who are you? Get out of here," said Mutobo, figuring John was an engineer his troops had missed in their sweeps.

"I am feeling pretty scared right now," said John reflexively.

"Join the club. How did my men miss you?"

"Um…I don't work here if that's what you're talking about. I'm John Rock."

"Holy shit! You are the friend of the big man. You need to get out of here, John. This bomb has less than seven minutes. If you refuse to leave, I'll shoot you. So get."

"That doesn't make any sense. You'd shoot me if I stayed? If I stay, the bomb will blow us up. So it doesn't matter. Game over." John really wanted to show Mutobo who was the smarter person in the room. "Lemme' guess, you're Mutobo and you finally have the UN and GU on their knees?"

"Yes. Get out of here. Leave, now!" yelled Mutobo as he cocked his pistol.

"I accept that I am feeling really scared. I accept unconditionally who I am but that doesn't mean I have to leave."

"What are you talking about? Leave me be, John Rock. I came here to die."

"Why?"

"What?"

"Why did you come here to die? When a person resigns themselves to death, they have chosen to stop thinking. They do not feel adequate to the challenge of self-responsibility. You have given up responsibility for yourself. I feel really sad about that. The thought is that you are a great leader and now you're giving it all up."

"I have nothing to live for," Mutobo said with a sob. He lowered his pistol.

"Have you seen Gemma Wayne?" asked John. He was feeling a little more brazen now that the gun in the room had been lowered.

"You came into this place to ask me if I have seen Gemma Wayne? She killed my family! She is the reason I am staying here in this dam. Without my family, there is nothing for me to live for. My strength is wasted. There will be no more golden sunsets for me. I am spent."

"I really hear your pain and I am sorry she hurt you. You didn't deserve that."

"Are you reading lines from a book? Who the fuck talks like that? I am spending my last moments with a madman!"

"Mutobo…it hurts when you make fun of me. Yes, I came here looking for Gemma Wayne. I actually wanted to bend her over doggy-style while she played my favorite game but I'm staying here because I can see you are conflicted. Sometimes when the sun is the darkest, we burn the brightest."

"No. There is nothing left. Without my wife and my daughter, I am nothing. The revolution can live on through Walter. He will stay in Zabon and carry on my legacy."

"What a burden for him!"

"What?"

"I'd say you're leaving your best friend with a terrible burden. You're taking the easy way out. You think that because your time is over on Earth that somehow people aren't going to experience the effects of your loss. Reality doesn't cease to exist just because your consciousness does. Come on, Tiger, that's Metaphysics 101."

"It's 'Lion', not 'Tiger'" Mutobo said spitefully.

"That's more like it!" beamed John. "Look, I can't change the decision you've made. You're a grown adult and have practiced your volition. All I am asking is that you see beyond your grief and try to imagine, just for a moment, the impact your death is going to have on everyone you leave behind. By the way, does Walter have a little bit of grey hair near his temples and really noticeable bifocals?"

"Yes. Why? Did you see him?"

"He was pinned down by some Blue Berets near the exit. I couldn't help him cause I don't use guns anymore. I'm a bomb expert."

"Where did you learn all these things? You talk like a scientist, act like a virgin boy, but somehow you speak the truth."

"I learned a lot of it from meditating on self-knowledge. A good dose of *Honest Communication* by the greatest philosopher of our time: Luke Fitzgibbons. And I have really good relationships with my best friends, Rupert and Arnold, that I built from first principles."

"I don't know what any of that means."

"Walter was alone."

"Oh my god!" yelled Mutobo as he jumped to his feet. "You're right. I can't leave my friend like that!"

"It would be selfish in the most negative sense of the word," offered John.

"You're really weird, man, but I like you. Let's get out of here."

"Wait a tick. You seriously haven't seen Gemma Wayne? I thought you kidnapped her."

"The last time I saw Gemma Wayne she was tied to a table in my room."

"You were going to fuck her?" asked John with a jealous intensity in his voice.

"That's crazy, man! I have a wife."

"You *had* a wife."

"What the fuck, John? Are you always like this?"

"We need to align our concepts with reality."

"I don't have time for this bullshit anymore. I'm leaving. You can come with me if you want. I'll protect you until we reach Walter, then you're on your own."

"Ah-ta-ta-ta," chided John. "I'm not letting that bomb go off."

"Then I'm going to have to shoot you"

"I'm feeling terror and the thought is you're going to shoot me. We can't let that bomb go off."

"You *are* with Gemma and the UN. The most bizarre negotiator I have ever seen. I'm staying here and making sure the bomb goes off."

"Don't be paranoid. Sorry. I didn't mean to inflict a conclusion there. I meant to say 'I am experiencing you as paranoid'"

"Are you trying to tell me that you are not with the UN? I'm confused."

"Now you're talking my language. What's the thought that comes with the confusion?"

"The bomb has three minutes. I don't have any more time for you, John. I'm going and you are coming with me," said Mutobo as he pointed the pistol in John's face.

John's eyes rolled into the back of his head and he took a deep breath. He summoned his Inner Hero.

"What I have to say is really important and it could change your life, Mutobo. Please take the gun out of my face and just give me 30 seconds more. I helped you see that your best friend needs you. Now I need you to see one more thing."

"Talk."

"Blowing up this dam is a huge mistake. Allow me to make the case. General Utility is a mega-multi-national corporation that is obviously propped up by the dying democracies of the world. They hemorrhage money on most of their projects and have their losses covered up by the printing presses of central banks. You know that. That's why you're here to blow this puppy up."

"Ten seconds."

"GU did market research on this one. The dam would be wildly profitable. Don't ask me how I know."

"You bought yourself another ten seconds."

"By blowing up the dam, you're blowing a huge opportunity to bring a bunch of wealth to the Bura and the Danta. Instead of destroying, you need to focus your efforts on ejecting the UN from the region and taking possession of the dam. Then you can auction off the dam to foreign parties and revitalize the local economy. Let me tell you, this mining boom is about to end. The Middle Eastern housing bubble is about to pop! They're not going to need your resources pretty soon."

"This makes sense. Fuck, John! We're out of time. We're fucked. You talked too long."

"What do you mean?"

"I can't switch off the bomb. The timer is below a minute."

"I can defuse it."

"That's impossible. I can't believe this. I'm going to die here with you because I listened to you talk for too long."

"At least you're taking personal responsibility for your behavior. That's a step in the right direction.'"

"I swear you have a formula for everything I'm going to say. Defuse the bomb and I'll try your plan."

Chapter 34

"These poor, broken children!" thought Arnold as he disarmed and knocked unconscious another pair of soldiers. The thought confused him for a moment. He settled into it and it began to feel natural. These were underdeveloped adults who had been starved of love and care as youngsters. Why else would they take up arms against each other and wade into battle? Arnold felt a reformation coming on, an enlightenment. The Powersuit had healed his brain. Why had it not healed the brain of the other man? The other man was slaughtering senselessly. Arnold had no answer as he ran through a ravine in pursuit of the sound of heavy weaponry.

A laser blast scorched the brush immediately next to him as he emerged into a clearing. It was the other Powersuit operator! He fired another shot at Arnold, almost in perfect anticipation of Arnold's evasive roll. A burning seared through his calf muscle and his HUD flashed red. He tackled the man to the ground, knocking the rifle far out of his hands. After a brief scuffle, Arnold had the man firmly in a choke hold and the man ceased to resist.

"Ease up," wheezed the man. "Let me say…something."

"Power down your Suit," growled Arnold.

The man promptly powered down, much to the displeasure of his viewing audience.

"There we are, mate. Right as rain. Now, are you the fellow that keeps disarming all of my prey? I'm losing a lot of money because of you!"

"You tried to kill me!"

"What? Aren't you a died-in-the-wool killer yourself?"

"Not anymore. Take the Suit off or I'll change my mind on snapping your neck." Arnold felt surprised at his sudden erudition. He released his grip on the man as the man slipped out of the Powersuit.

"Where's John?" he asked the man.

"That sniveling prick who ripped the balls off one of our men? I haven't the slightest. Poof. Gone for all I know. We lost a couple of helicopters. He was shackled to one, maybe one of the ones we lost."

Jason felt very uncomfortable with the lack of electronic voices broadcasting into his head.

"Why did the Suit change me? I used to be dumb."

"Ah! That's my special "III" version of the suit, equipped with the most advanced medical equipment on the planet. The only other one like it is that one," he said as he pointed to the Suit he had just shorn. "Cost me…well, let's just say more than Coca Cola profits in one year. Fuck me, I wish I hadn't shot a hole in it."

"You're equivocating. Answer me."

"It didn't change you for any particular reason. One simply puts it on and eventually has cellular reconstruction done on several key parts of the body: your liver, your heart, your brain, and your lungs."

"It healed me and now I cannot kill. Why are you still killing? Didn't you wear it?"

"It did indeed heal you. Apparently your brain was in much need of some reconstruction. Effects from a nasty childhood, eh?"

"My parents beat me severely. How did you know?"

"Beatings and verbal abuse tend to accumulate brain damage. You lose impulse control to an astonishing degree. Hold on. You're with John Rock. You're Arnold Colfax! We did quite the background check on you. You were a savage killer. I had a sneaking suspicion you were behind the patrol ambush yesterday near Mutobo's."

"I am not killing again. What I did yesterday was awful."

"Cheer up, mate. What you did could bring you money. Loads of it!"

"Why do you kill? Answer me."

"I kill because I make the choice to. A healed brain has given me so much: power, fortune, fame, sex, and all the thrills a warm-blooded man could want. I navigate through this world that glorifies violence as a near demi god. Healed brain or not, I still retain the power to choose. I choose to kill because it affords me my lifestyle. There's no good or evil. There's matter and no moral directive can be derived from it. I am a stable collection of atoms and nothing more. Questions of morality ceased to exist for me when I had the reconstruction. You are the only other person to receive the Suit's process. Even the finest labs in Shanghai can't reproduce the reconstruction on the scale that I have. We are gods now, Arnold!"

"You're a monster."

"That's quite a claim to level. Prove it to me."

"I don't have time. I need to find John."

"John's fine. His helicopter left for base. He's probably in a holding cell somewhere. Between you and me, this battle is completely over anyway. Everyone's either dead or tied to a tree. Come on, prove your claim."

A UN soldier ran into the clearing, noticed the Powersuits, and sprinted away as fast as he could.

"It's sounding and looking like we've got a little bit of time, what do you say?" asked Jason.

"Fine. Do you accept that there is nothing distinguishing you on a biological level from other humans?"

"Other than nearly-perfect vital organs? No, there's nothing distinguishing me from others on a biological level."

"We're not gods then?"

"No, that was simply a figure of speech."

"I'll proceed. If there's nothing biologically distinguishable from you and the rest of humanity, can we then say that theories for human behavior apply to you as equally as they do to others?"

"Yes."

"Wow, I did not expect you to answer that! You've mostly been equivocating up until now."

"I'm interested in seeing where your Socratic questioning is going."

"Thank you for that courtesy. Ten minutes ago you were wholesale slaughtering your fellow man. Okay, back to where we were. Do you accept the validity of theories such as the theory of gravity?"

"Naturally."

"Are there theories for human behavior that are universal for all humans?"

"Like Maslow's Hierarchy of Needs? Those kind of theories?"

"More or less," Arnold paused and thought back on all the things that John had taught him. It all seemed to come back to him with perfect clarity.

"You have posited there is no morality, no indicators of universally preferable behavior for humans to be found in nature," said Arnold.

"Don't you mean 'preferred'?"

"Preferred would indicate that, if we talking about universal across all humans, everyone already prefers these terms for human morality. This is not the case. 'Preferable' recognizes that the conditions of the system of ethics I'm about to propose is something that people can attain but not necessarily already possess in their thinking."

"That's an interesting interpretation between the terms. I'm sure some would find fault in it but I'm going to stick with this and see where you go with it."

"Again, your courtesy in the face of all this carnage is astonishing."

"Please…I'm disarmed. Let's not forget the circumstances." Jason waved a dismissive hand.

"You're right. Shall I? If you accept that there can be universal theories for human behavior, that all humans are similar on a biological level, let's do a little experiment. How about physical aggression, for example?"

Other than some scattered gunfire and an occasional explosion, all was silent for Walter. No explosion had come from the dam. Concurrent thoughts of Mutobo's mission failure and the question of Gemma's presence ran through Walter's head. Should he press forward and see if his last two grenades had finished her and her squad off? Should he retreat to check on Mutobo and possibly allow any surviving UN forces to advance on the dam entrance?

His questions were answered for him as Mutobo emerged from the dam with a slender white man wearing khaki slacks and a burgundy collared shirt. They had their arms draped over each other's shoulders and were laughing and joking as though they were old friends. Walter had never seen Mutobo so friendly with a white man before. It also struck him as very odd that they would not be on the lookout for danger.

"Walta'! This is John Rock. The man who saved my life. Please, shake hands."

Walter approached them and beckoned them to duck down.

"Gemma Wayne and a whole lot of Blue Berets are just beyond those offices."

"Did you kill her?" asked John as he and Walter shook hands.

"I have not heard anything for the last three or four minutes. No signs of an advance. It's too quiet elsewise. I don't have a good feeling about this, Lion. John, I have heard some things about you from our people in Ulako. Is it true? Do you walk around your plantation in nothing but white underwear?"

"That's how I roll. You game?"

"When I was a boy. Why is the dam intact? We should all be dead right now!"

"John came in to the turbine room, looking for Gemma Wayne. Can you believe he was going to try and fuck her?"

"I had the thought myself," chuckled Walter.

"Thanks, man. That's really affirming to hear from another intellectual," John piped in just as Mutobo was going to speak again. "Often I find that the good choices I make from a place of self-knowledge are mirrored back to me by other great mean. Ms. Wayne, though, is not all she seems to purport herself as. Mu can attest to it."

Mutobo continued on with his report.

"So I'm sitting there with the deepest pain in my heart, watching the bomb tick away and keeping my wife and daughter close to my thoughts, and this strange white man crawls out of the wall."

"Well- not strange but self-possessed-"

"I don't remember how he did it, Walta', but he convinced me that dying with the dam was a self-sacrifice. By dying, I would do more harm and let Gemma Wayne win. She is our common enemy. I told him about her murdering and now here we are."

"Sir, we are in the middle of a battlefield and so much conversation is not safe. We have no reports from the field. Please, let's save this for HQ."

"You're right. We need to fan out and determine the situation. Rock, are you versed with sidearms?"

"Versed but don't touch em'. I don't use guns."

"One last thing, Lion: why is the dam still standing?"

"Simple. This dam is going to be wildly profitable. I trust John in what he is saying about their research. I don't know why. It's my intuition guiding me here. We're in possession of it, for now. We can wield their own tools against them. We can oust our enemies through economic means. The renminbi is more powerful than the rifle."

A lone figure stumbled out from cover into sight. John took up a defensive Combat Pilates stance. The two freedom fighters drew and trained their pistols. It was Gemma Wayne. She was missing an arm. Her other arm was raised in surrender. Her fire squads were scattered on the ground behind her, each in pools of blood.

"You have got to be shitting me," said John through pursed lips.

"Down on the ground!" barked Walter as he approached her with his pistol trained on her chest.

She obliged him through sobs and cries of pain. Mutobo tore part of her light jacket away in order to make a tourniquet for the stub of her left arm. As he prepared the tourniquet, Gemma began to speak.

"My arm…it's gone. My men are all dead. Why?"

"Those who live by the sword die by the sword," gloated John.

"Take it easy, Mr. Rock," said Mutobo. "She is missing her arm and probably has lost some of her hearing."

"You're telling me to take it easy? You're not my dad! Besides, she killed your family, dude."

Mutobo ignored the "dad" comment.

"Our mission must change. From now on our rebellion must be committed to compassion and entrepreneurship. I have you to thank for that."

Almost reflexively, John said, "You're right. Fitzgibbons teaches us that compassion is the *second* virtue and that entrepreneurship is the *seventh*. Not a bad pair of virtues to try and pursue with integrity. Personally, I live for the first virtue and the fourth. It's a more balanced approach considering my historical trajectory and the fact that I have an apprentice."

Walter joined in on the conversation and soon Gemma Wayne was an afterthought to another meeting of minds.

"Are you talking about Luke Fitzgibbons?"

"Yeah, why? Is that a problem?"

"No, no, no, not at all. Fitzgibbons is one of the greatest philosophers of all time. The ripples of his unifying theory of ethics are still expanding and changing the world today."

"I feel happy and the thought is that you are another philosopher," John said formulaically.

"I feel pleased and the thought is that I have found another person to be vulnerable with," responded Walter.

Mutobo wrinkled his nose at the two and stepped away, unnoticed, to smoke a cigarette he had taken from Gemma's jacket.

"Hey assholes!" Gemma called from her spot on the ground.

"Not now, Ms. Wayne," said Walter. "We are communicating in real time."

She eyed them as though they were mad physicists. Her shock was wearing off and her arm was starting to burn with a hellfire second only to her errant miscarriage as a teenager long before.

"Fuck this," she said out loud to herself. She rolled onto her back and sat up. She gathered her strength and stood up. Mutobo noticed her and butted out his cigarette.

"Let me walk you to a medic," he offered.

"Why haven't you killed me? You know what I did."

"I suppose I am justified in killing you, aren't I? I am not going to. That Mr. Rock is a strange man but he convinced me that the bloodshed must stop. Business and caring for others must take the place of the violence. I have made a vow to never kill again, even if it means I can never avenge my family. That is a terrible wound that will take years to heal and killing you won't help me get closure. Your death would be more blood on my hands and I have had enough, not another drop."

"You're not going to have me executed? Are you fucking crazy?"

"I am crazy, Ms. Wayne, and so are you. We're all very sick people. We run around with guns and duties and trample thousands of people underfoot for our own desires. I touched the face of God back in that dam and this is what I saw. The Lion is no more. We need to go to a hospital or something. Everyone here is dead."

"Christmas…"

"What?"

"Jason Christmas."

"He's here?"

"Last I saw. We contracted him to help us bring you down. He got a bunch of sponsors to go on a killing spree. He's why everyone is dead."

"You didn't stop him?"

"No. I cheered him on."

"How can you live with yourself, Ms. Wayne?"

"I am dead inside, Mutobo. You really should kill me. I'll kill again. It's all I know."

Mutobo stopped walking and Gemma did the same. He looked her in the eyes for the first time since she was captive in his hut.

"You are correct. You are dead inside. That's why we cannot execute you."

Walter and John caught up. It was obvious they had been arguing about something. Mutobo smiled to himself at the nonsense these intellectuals could stir up. They all turned their attention to Gemma.

"I thought I was in love with you but now I can see it was you actually having a strong personality and influencing me the way my mother used to," blurted John.

"You never had a chance. My arm is fucking blown off and all you bastards want to do is talk to each other and try to teach me things. My arm isn't attached anymore? Hello?"

"Her inner child is throwing a tantrum. Don't worry, guys," said John.

"I'm not familiar to what you're referring to but I feel curious and the thought is 'There are many intellectual conversations to come'. Right now we need to see to it that she gets medical care. We need to assess the battlefield. There may be survivors and we owe them our full efforts," said Walter as he pushed his pistol into Gemma's back and beckoned the others to walk with them.

"Let's not treat her like that," suggested Mutobo. "Our enemies will now be met with dignity and compassion."

"I swear to God I am surrounded by weirdoes wherever I go in Africa," growled Ms. Wayne.

"You're really inflicting us with your conclusions, Gemma," John whined.

"Okay, I'm going to play your guys' stupid logic games. John Rock, or whatever the fuck you call yourself, telling me I'm inflicting conclusions is in itself a conclusion. You're a huge hypocrite. Now cut out the crap. Either get me a medic or put a bullet in my skull. I'm tired of listening to you try to convince everyone you've got it all together with this enlightened communication crap. Both you and me know that you've got some mommy issues that you're trying to pass off on others."

John began to appeal to the two men with him. "This is exactly what Luke Fitzgibbons warns us against when we enter into relationships with-" Gemma cut him off swiftly.

"If you talk one more time while I'm around, I will literally shove my bloody stump into your face and make you taste how pissed off I am right now!"

John stopped walking and his eyes rolled into the back of his head. The others glanced back at him as they continued on in search of some sort of medical supply. He took a deep breath and shuddered in a way that wracked his whole body. Suddenly he was beaming and whistling. He followed his companions at a distance. They were all very annoyed by his behavior but said nothing.

They weaved through splattered bodies of UN soldiers and occasional rebel corpses. The UN forces were nearly all decimated by Jason Christmas or the precision tactics of rebel lieutenants. A few who remained alive and either bound to trees or pinned to the ground with netting from Arnold's Powersuit considered calling out to Gemma Wayne for help until they saw the Lion himself guiding her as a captive to some unknown destination. They feigned unconsciousness for fear of being executed by the pistol of the ferocious warrior, Walter.

The group was very fortunate in that the first bound rebel they came upon was Stephen, a med student and volunteer field medic for larger scale operations.

"Is everyone dead?" he asked as he was being untied.

"We have only seen a few UN men alive," said Mutobo.

"This place is a graveyard, otherwise," volunteered John.

"Marcus was with me but something dropped down on us. I saw a flash of red and then nothing. I woke up and have been waiting."

"Where is Marcus?" asked Walter.

"Sir, I don't know. Assim is over there though. He says it was a big man in a Powersuit. I don't know what that is. He saw him tying everyone up and taking their guns."

Stephen was unbound and began treating Gemma's wound as well as he could. He was ordered to help Assim and then reconnaissance the area for other rebel survivors. There were no weapons to be found anywhere.

"Are there reinforcements coming?" Mutobo asked Gemma. He was going to send her away with a pair of rebel guards to await trial at the rebel base.

"We sent everyone."

"I want confirmation of this. Find us a communicator, now," he said to Walter and three other subordinates.

"Take her away. Do not harm a hair on her head," he ordered the two stupefied escorts.

As she was being taken away, John spoke to her one last time, "If you get out of prison and are still fertile, I might be available or at least willing to fool around…"

She lashed out at him and rubbed her bloody stump on his face before passing out into the arms of her guards from the exertion. John took off in a dead sprint toward the Bura River. He was rubbing the entire contents of a travel-sized bottle of hand sanitizer on his face and coughing.

The day was ending and no further UN reinforcements left their main base. There were none to send. The rebels and United Nations soldiers had largely cancelled each other out with bullets. Those that did survive the slaughter were subject to the rampage of Jason Christmas or the loving punches to the temple from Arnold Colfax. Villagers from the valley cautiously streamed into the dam area to reclaim their loved ones. Night fell. Gemma Wayne was placed in a cell with all the amenities a decimated rebel militia could afford her. Powerful painkillers beckoned her to slumber. Walter busied himself with recovery of survivors and the burial of fallen comrades. He stroked his beard in the brief moments he allowed himself to feel the sadness that was to overcome him for many months to come. There was no drive left in him to soldier. All that was left was his sadness and the desire to have some sort of positive effect on the families torn apart by the battle. He committed himself to supporting Mutobo's bid of making the dam profitable for a large ownership group of locals. Mutobo wept in the shadows of a building before gathering the strength to ensure the seizure of the dam and the dispersal of his rebel group. His life became a tribute to non-violence.

Charlie and Joanna tripped through the entire battle. When they began to sense that their bodies were getting cold, they rose up and stumbled along a beaten path through the jungle. Eventually they were discovered by a villager on his way to Ulako. They spent the night in the Aubame brothel. Sobriety didn't reach them for two more days. They were on a flight back home within the week. Charlie became a trained psychotherapist. Joanna continued to work in hospitals for little to no pay.

Chapter 35

John Rock fell asleep on a river rock jutting out from the Bura. His legs lay in a puddle of his own vomit. His eyes flickered back and forth as he dreamt.

"Mom, I thought I beat you but you've been here this whole time haven't you?" he asked himself in the mirror of his plantation hut. A ghostly figure stepped from the reflection of the mirror into the air around him. It was the mystery man from his Fizzle match.

"Do you know who I am?" asked the man.

"Kind of. Didn't we face off in Fizzle or something? Why did you step out of me?"

"John, listen closely. I'm you from the future. I'm who you could become if you listen to my wisdom. Whether you listen or not is up to you. You have free choice in this."

"You're not in charge of this conversation, mister. I am. Did I beat you at Fizzle or not?"

"Of course you beat me, John. You're much more practiced at this point than I am. You did a marvelous job and I really appreciated the match. Good for you!"

John studied the man up and down. His dream started to fade but he rubbed his palms together to stay in it. The mystery man was no longer wearing a mullet. For some reason, this made John very happy. Some joyous insight bubbled up within in him and his whole disposition toward the man changed.

"That's it, buddy. You get it, don't you?" asked the man knowingly.

"Yes! I get it now. You're the leader here aren't you?"

"Bingo! You've got that right."

"Wow! You even talk like me. Is this your mirror?"

"Everything here is mine but I'll share whatever you want. Our time together is short. You're going to wake up soon. You can feel it, right?"

John rubbed his palms together one last time. He wasn't going to be able to maintain the dream for much longer.

"I'm all ears."

"That's wonderful, John. Congratulations on saving the life of the Lion and for resisting Ms. Wayne. The Lion was lost and on the edge of death. Ms. Wayne was the perfect storm of your history. You changed their lives forever with your light of truth. What I'm going to say to you now is super important. Can you listen just a little more?"

John nodded his head. He was wearing a birthday hat and sitting in front of a large cake with a plastic monster truck in the center.

"There is a very deep place inside of you that is hurting. It influences all of your behavior. It's why you can't get a real girlfriend. It's why people feel very uncomfortable around you sometimes. Can you see it?"

John nodded his head again and felt a deep urge to blow out the candles on the cake.

"Not just yet. I'm going to give you the first clue and you're going to have to sort it out from there. The next time you are meditating, I want you to meditate on the phrase 'fear of abandonment'. Can you do that for me, sweet John?"

John began to blubber as something deep inside of him awoke and fussed.

"You've done so well, John. You helped so many people in a very true way. Now you can relax and begin to change. Your work is done, in a sense. There's something fussing. Better blow out those candles now. Don't forget the golden clue."

Arnold stood over John as he came to his senses. Arnold peered down at his friend from the comfort of his newly acquired Powersuit IV.

"Where have you been? I thought you were still at the plantation," began John, expecting the usual stony silence from Arnold.

"It's a long story."

"Hold up. Did you just talk? When did you start talking again? You haven't talked in months!"

"It's the Suit, Johnny. It healed me. It healed my brain. Now I talk. Actually, I can do much more than that!"

"Whoa, buddy! I want one too."

"You're just in luck. I'm wearing the IV, you can have the III. I ran back to the plantation and stored it in your hut for you."

"You *ran* back to the plantation?"

"Yeah! This thing lets me run up to 100 miles per hour. The III can get 95. Hurts like hell to hit a tree but if you chart your route you're usually okay."

John was dumbfounded for the first time in his life. He studied Arnold in the Powersuit and took inventory of the scenery around him. He tensed up a little.

"Why do you get the IV and I only get the III? You're the apprentice, remember?"

"Not anymore, John. We're equals now. According to this thing's OS, most of my brain trauma is cleared up. There are some deep pockets neither of the Suits can reach but its way better than nothing. Now I have restored to me all of the cognitive processes that were robbed from me through the brain traumas I've sustained throughout the year. You taught me well but now I can actually do my own thinking. I don't have to lug around the plantation like a chunk of meat and do a bunch of drugs if somehow my conscience starts to slur into view. It's all different. Even my worldview has changed."

"I think mine has too. I think I semi-accidentally may have done some really good things today. There's some serious dream journaling ahead of me. Oh no-no-no-no, my LTS is busted!"

"Where you're going, friend, you're not going to need the LTS anymore," Arnold said as he gave John a confident smile.

"Did you kill Jason Christmas and jack his Suits?"

"Funny thing: we ended up debating for the better part of an hour and a half. Most of the dead combatants you see around here are his doing. I disarmed him and tried reasoning with him. He's got a heavy dose of that quicksand nihilism going on-"

"Oh, that shit," groaned John as he stood up and grimaced at the vomit staining his pleated khakis.

"-you know it. We had it out for a while and basically it came down to him admitting there could be universal standards for ethics but then hedging and hedging with allusions to our superior physiological conditions as products of the healing process of the Powersuit. Guy was really caught up on some sort of 'ubermensch' mentality. Like, 'Come on, dude. Read some Fitzgibbons or some at least some Rothbard!' I sat down funny and accidentally switched on the Suit's data feed. Saw that we basically have clemency if we do a couple product endorsements. Christmas Media negotiated me into a show contract on the promise that I wouldn't kill their CEO. I demanded the Suits, too."

"You didn't kill him?"

"Why kill him when Christmas Media would just hunt us to the ends of the Earth for revenge?"

"Good point. You really have graduated from apprentice!"

They were nearing the plantation when Arnold sighed woefully.

"Rupert ran away," he said.

"I feel pretty sad right now."

"You know something, that's the first time you've spoken in real time and I've actually believed you were being sincere."

"Thanks," sniffled John. "Do you think he'll come back?"

"Probably, that stupid cat always finds a way back home."

They stepped onto the plantation grounds and began a new life as equals.

ENJOY THE BOOK?

Leave it a review on Amazon and Goodreads.

Made in the USA
Columbia, SC
21 November 2020